PENGUIN BOOKS

THE PRISONER

THOMAS M. DISCH is the author of more than twenty books and twelve collections of poetry. He is widely regarded as one of the masters of twentieth-century science fiction, and received many nominations and awards throughout his career, including the 1999 Hugo Award for his book *The Dreams Our Stuff Is Made Of: How Science Fiction Conquered the World*. He died in 2008.

THE PRISONER

THOMAS M. DISCH

PENGUIN BOOKS

PENGUIN BOOKS

Published by the Penguin Group
Penguin Group (USA) Inc., 375 Hudson Street, New York, New York 10014, U.S.A.
Penguin Group (Canada), 90 Eglinton Avenue East, Suite 700, Toronto,
Ontario, Canada M4P 2Y3 (a division of Pearson Penguin Canada Inc.)
Penguin Books Ltd, 80 Strand, London WC2R 0RL, England
Penguin Ireland, 25 St Stephen's Green, Dublin 2, Ireland
(a division of Penguin Books Ltd)
Penguin Group (Australia), 250 Camberwell Road, Camberwell,
Victoria 3124, Australia (a division of Pearson Australia Group Pty Ltd)
Penguin Books India Pvt Ltd, 11 Community Centre,
Panchsheel Park, New Delhi – 110 017, India
Penguin Group (NZ), 67 Apollo Drive, Rosedale, North Shore 0632,
New Zealand (a division of Pearson New Zealand Ltd)
Penguin Books (South Africa) (Pty) Ltd, 24 Sturdee Avenue,
Rosebank, Johannesburg 2196, South Africa

Penguin Books Ltd, Registered Offices:
80 Strand, London WC2R 0RL, England

First published in the United States of America by
Carlton International Media Limited 1967
Published in Penguin Books 2009

1   3   5   7   9   10   8   6   4   2

ISBN 978-0-14-311722-3

Printed in the United States of America

To Jane
and
to Pamela:
in equal shares

Contents

THE PRISONER

PART I

ARRIVAL

I have been studying how I may compare
This prison where I live unto the world.

Shakespeare, *Richard II*

Chapter One

The Connaught

"Have you been here before?" he asked.

"Wasn't it here that we came, the last time?"

"Not possibly. We were last together in . . . Trier, if my memory serves."

"Mine, apparently, does not. Coming across you again, everything gets very déjà vu. The chandeliers, the flowers, even that waiter with the Hapsburg lip. They're all exactly the way I remember them."

"If this is what your déjà vu's are made of, you've had an agreeable past."

"Small thanks to you, darling."

He touched her empty glass. "Once more?"

"Didn't you say you were in a terrible rush? Besides, it wouldn't show respect for the bisque. Which is already gliding to our table."

The waiter with the Hapsburg lip performed deft rituals with the bisque, while they, with the preliminary skirmish over, made minor modifications in their strategies. The wine steward brought the Solera, its brittle label flaking from the glass.

"Yes," he said. "Then, with the salmon, Coindreu Chateau Grillet."

"And I've seen *him* before too," she said. "Did you notice the funny ring he was wearing. No, men never notice how other men dress. It's delicious. If the venison is half so nice, I'll marry you. Would you like that?"

"I might. I've never had a wife."

"I'd make a very attractive wife for you, I think. You'd never have to feel embarrassed. I speak French, German, Polish, and probably something else. As I have my own income, I wouldn't even be expensive–except at Christmas–though I'd *look* expensive all the time. Whenever your self-confidence faltered–"

"It doesn't."

"–my skilful flattery would bolster you up. And I'm not *too* much younger. Am I?"

"Not at all."

"Do you fear I'd be too frivolous? Do you take exception to the coloratura passages? You, if anyone, should realize that my serious side is *just* as serious as yours. Make a serious face. Oh, like that! All those wrinkles–the strength of character they suggest."

"It's the supraorbital ridge that does that."

"It's so many things."

"You have good points too."

"Each complements one of yours. Imagine the two of us walking into the same room. We're surrounded with whispers, the cynosure of all men's eyes. The waltz swells about us, and you take me in your arms."

"What are they whispering?"

"That you're forty years old, and still single."

"Thirty-eight."

"*C'est la même*, darling. We'll both have little secrets tucked away in dresser drawers, behind our stockings. I would have thought forty more likely."

"You listen too much to the things people whisper."

"Let's leave them, then. They mean nothing to *us*. We'll go off by ourselves. To the Seychelle Islands? Meshed? The Philippines? They're said to be quite in now."

"We won't listen to what people say. We value our independence too highly."

"Where shall we go, then? You tell me."

"To Wales."

"Oh, not Wales! One must draw a line between independence and ennui."

"I've already signed the papers, love. I am committed."

"This isn't pretending, then?"

"I hope not, after all the money I've sunk in it."

"Where in Wales?"

"The Pembroke coast. It has one of the quaintest names on the map."

"Oh, I know just what it will look like–all the cottages built out of marzipan, and an abbey church from the 14th century, the rustics brawling in the pub, fishing boats, sunsets. You'll live in somebody's converted toolshed."

"A gatehouse, actually. I leased it through Chandler & Carr."

"Who showed you photographs."

"And a floor plan."

"Though smallish, it possesses every convenience."

"A majority, at least."

"I don't believe it. It isn't you. What about your *work*?"

He paused at this, the first point scored in the game.

"I've retired."

"I *don't* believe it. You? Though, of course, if that's what you're supposed to *say*..."

"It's been my impression that it's not at all what I was supposed to say. But I do say it, I have done it, I am retired."

"Why, in God's name?"

"That's a secret I've tucked away in a dresser drawer, behind my stockings."

Which tied it, one all.

"And the dresser? Off in the rural, implausible solitudes of Pembroke?"

"Still in London, most likely. I only bought it today. That's why we met here. I've been up and down Bond Street all day, furnishing the place."

"And *not* because we're so convenient to Grosvenor Square?"

"I thought that might make it handier for you."

"They won't buy it, you know. You can't just go and tell them you've lost interest in the whole thing, for heaven's sake!"

"On the contrary, Liora—you *can*."

"You called me Liora. That was nice of you."

"It's your name."

"It's not the name on my passport. You are a darling, and you really do believe in integrity and honor and all of that. Yes, thank you, just a wee bit more. 1872! And without an expense account?" When the steward had left them, she continued: "Is that what you'd call a Masonic ring?"

"I forgot to look."

"He also uses wax on his mustache. I've never kissed a waxed mustache. Remember where you kissed me, in Bergamo?"

"That was where I didn't kiss you."

A palpable hit. He moved into the lead.

"But you wanted to. Why are you looking seriously now? Is it about me?"

"Yes."

"No, it isn't. You're having second thoughts about all that furniture. What did you get? Where? How much did they make you pay?"

He itemized on his fingers. "Four Chinese Chippendale chairs, at Mallett's. A mahogany table from J. Cornelius, that copies one at the South Kensington. A Sirhaz carpet in the pear design. A Riesener secretaire that's very much restored. Oh, and odds and ends. I forget how much—"

"Fantasy, all of it."

"I did see them, and I might have wanted them. Actually I just picked out some bare essentials at Liberty's. Here's the salmon."

Bare and essential, the salmon was presented. The Coindreu was open, tasted, and approved. Richebourg '29 was suggested for the impending venison Diane. Their conversation, set against the backdrop of this restaurant, this meal, seemed to lack the element of chance. The ordered sequence of dishes dictated not only the wines they drank but also the words they spoke and the glances that passed between them. Even their errors were such as only the most expert players could have made.

Her serve.

"What do you intend to *do* in Wales? Fish? Think? Write your memoirs? Discover some new inner resource, or a hobby?"

"What's customary for a country gentlemen these days?"

"Alcoholism."

Which might have tied the score again, if the glance that accompanied it had not, so noticeably, grazed the net. She tried again.

"When do you leave?"

"From Paddington, at half past eleven."

"Tonight?"

He nodded.

"How ridiculous! You asked me here . . . just to have dinner . . . and to tell me that you're leaving town?"

"I thought you'd enjoy eating out, and that you'd want to say goodbye."

"You don't give me time to say much else. I'd hoped . . . Well, you knew what I hoped."

"You didn't hope. You took for granted."

He had moved lengths ahead of her: she was reduced to being forthright.

"Why *did* you want to see me? You won't say you love me, and you won't say you don't. You sit there and decorate yourself with wrinkles and irony. You know, if you can't trust *me*, you'll never be able to trust anyone. You sit there with your enigma dangling in front of you like some fat gold watch chain. You're just inviting someone to grab it my dear."

She leaned back in her chair, touching the emerald pendant on her throat, while these points were added to her score.

The waiter with the Hapsburg lip replaced the china on the table according to a strict and clandestine geometry. The dinner approached its climax.

"Do you think I look Jewish?" she asked.

"You look dark and mysterious. Your face expresses great strength of character."

"And you won't postpone your trip just one night?"

"There isn't a pullman every night. I'm sorry, Liora–I've made up my mind."

"Someone has–that's certain."

But the game was clearly his, for all that. She smiled, conceding it, and began to talk about nothing at all.

When they left the restaurant, at ten forty-five, the waiter with the Hapsburg lip, ignoring more pressing demands, cleared the cups and Tokaj glasses from the table. He pursed his mouth at the flower vase, from which the dark-haired woman had purloined the single rose.

He replaced the linen cloth with one slightly crisper, and on this, beside the new flowers, he put the small wooden plaque that indicated, in incised, gilt letters, the number of this table-6.

Chapter Two

A Round Trip to Cheltenham

The two identical Hartmann Knocabouts stood, already packed, beneath the false mirror in the foyer, like a demonstration of one of the less obvious axioms devised by the Alexandrian geometers. In the reception room the butler, a dumb and slightly Oriental dwarf, pressed the button that released the ornamental screen: he entered. The butler handed him his gloves.

"The telephone?" he asked.

In reply the butler removed the receiver from its cradle and offered it, as mute as himself, across the intervening space. Dead.

"Very good. The Locust is at the garage, I take it?" The butler nodded. "There's no particular hurry. When they've finished you can drive it on to Carmarthen. Wire me from there."

He turned for a last survey of the room. Depersonalized by dust covers, the furniture could not evoke so much as a flicker of sentimental regret. Like the monolithic pavilions of a defunct World's Fair, the room seemed already to be impatient for its own era of privacy, decay, and picturesque abandonment.

His fingers wriggled into kid gloves. Now there must be some gesture of departure, the closing of curtains, keys in locks. The butler stood at the opposite end of the room; he removed, from a pocket of his waistcoat, a key, turned, fitted it into the glass door of the bookshelves, turned the key.

"Not," he said, "the Dickens."

Obediently the butler reached, on tiptoe, to the fourth shelf and removed a slim sextodecimo volume of frayed morocco. Relocked the shelves. Crossed the room, padding on bare parquet, offered the book to its owner.

"Yes, that will do nicely." He slipped it in the pocket of his raincoat. "Goodbye, then."

The butler lifted a pudgy white-gloved hand and waved goodbye.

In the foyer he dipped his knees, caught a handle in each hand, and rose with the weight of the suitcases. The steel screen purred shut, sealing his past. He kicked open the front door. The taxi was waiting, aglow in the drizzle.

"Paddington," he said.

"It's fifteen after eleven, sir. No trains are running now."

"My train leaves at eleven-thirty."

The driver shrugged, and lifted the flag of the meter, which ticked off sixpences and fractions of miles along the Brompton Road, through Knightsbridge and past the flood-lit Corinthian columns of Apsley House, turning left and turning left again along the perimeter of Hyde Park, then right into Gloucester Terrace.

The station clock said eleven-thirty.

"Thank you, sir. Thank you very much."

He walked with his two bags toward Gate 6. A blue-uniformed ticket puncher waved at him, across the intervening space, to hurry. But for the two of them, the station looked as deserted as a cathedral in one of those counties tourists never find. Liora had carried on about her cathedrals, Salisbury, Winchester, Wells, all through the bombes.

While the man worried the ticket with his punch, he glanced backward, thinking he had seen her. It was only a young American, in army surplus, seated on a knapsack, her back propped against the Sherwood green tin of W. H. Smith's, sleeping or seeming to sleep.

The conductor was waiting outside the blue sleeping car to help him with his bags. Before he had been shown to his compartment, the train had begun to move.

"I will arrive . . . ?"

The conductor glanced at the destination hand-written on the ticket. "At half past six. The engine is changed once in Bristol and again in Swansea."

He found the bed in his compartment already made, the sheet spread back to receive his body, the pillow plumped. He drew the blinds. He removed his raincoat, his gloves.

He began to read:

Escalus.

My Lord.

Of government the properties to unfold . . .

On the small screen in his own compartment, the conductor watched the swaying man turn the pages of his little book. Often, to his distress, he would turn them backward instead of forward, but not so often, after all, that he did not reach the end. He then rose, swaying, and began to undress, unknotting, first, the black bow tie, prying off the cufflinks from his cuffs. He shrugged out of the jacket, loosed the cummerbund, slipped the suspenders from his shoulders, unbuttoned his fly, stepped out of the trousers.

He hung trousers, jacket, shirt inside the closet of simulated wood, placed tie, cummerbund and cufflinks on the shelf above. He lifted the handle of the door to LOCK.

Then he moved for a moment out of range of the closed-circuit camera. The microphone picked up the sound of running water. He returned, naked now, to the bed and pulled the upper sheet loose. The conductor, who, though probably no older than this man, could no longer think of himself as fit, had time briefly to admire the sturdiness of these limbs, the trimness of the torso. Then the light blanked.

"The second camera," a voice commanded.

The conductor adjusted a knob at the side of the screen. It now showed a man's head, cradled in his hands, swaying. He stared directly at the lens concealed in the ceiling for several minutes. Even when his eyes had closed, his face did not seem to relax. It was a quarter past two.

The conductor picked up his copy of *News of the World* and read the captions beneath each picture. At a quarter to three, a buzzer, at E-flat frequency, brought him to his feet.

The man was now asleep.

The conductor flipped up the switch marked VENT beneath the screen and watched as the mask descended over the man's face. When the mask was retracted, the facial muscles at last showed some degree of relaxation.

He went into the corridor and pulled the EMERGENCY cord. He unlocked the upper half of the door, reached in, turned the handle down to OPEN.

He pulled the slack, naked, fit body out of the bed. Twelve cars ahead the engine whistled. He stood low for a better grip beneath the armpits. The floor lurched.

Four men had gathered in the corridor. They watched the conductor pulling the man across the beige Acrilan without offering to help. Lights flickered by outside the windows. The train was approaching Cheltenham well ahead of schedule. It came to a full stop by the siding of a cable warehouse. While the four men unloaded the limp body on to the boards of the siding, the conductor returned to the compartment for the two suitcases, and again for the clothes and the copy of *Measure for Measure*. There was barely time to place these on the platform before the train was moving again. Spools of heavy cable flicked past *accelerando*. The four men returned, each to his own compartment.

The conductor tidied the mussed bed, plumped the pillow, scoured the sink.

At Cheltenham the engine was switched. By four o'clock the string of cars was rolling back home to Paddington. Lights cut long arcs through the incessant drizzle.

Chapter Three

The Village

Woke.

Soft Muzak, sore limbs. He flicked flecks of sleep from the corners of his eyes. He was awake now. His shoes confronted him, propped on the two identical suitcases. Laces dangled from the eyelets.

He patted his breast pocket. He stood up. The cummerbund, unbuckled, slid down his wrinkled legs. The Muzak glided into *Oklahoma*.

The entire room–varnished benches, sooty windows, overheated air, the worn, well-swept floorboards, the twin slates for Arrivals and Departures, the ticking clock, the thick, inverted L of the stovepipe leading to the stove–was transparently probable.

It was, by this clock, III minutes after IX, a statement that the light slanting through the grimy lattice confirmed. CLOSED hung lopsides before the ticket window grille. Oh, what a beautiful morning!

There was one Arrival, at 6:30 am. There were no Departures.

He went out onto the platform, into the incontrovertible likelihood of sunlight, cirrus clouds, the scent of creosote. A white wooden planter, Property of the Village, welcomed him to . . . ? For the entire length of the platform there was no sign to say. Well, to the Village then, in its most absolute sense.

He knotted his shoelaces, and in front of the mirror that sold chewing gum he tied a bow knot in his bow tie. His hair was not mussed by sleep. The cummerbund went into his raincoat pocket.

He returned to the platform with his suitcases and followed the arrows to TAXIS. A gravel path hedged with rhododendrons curved to the back of the station and debouched on a street of devastating neatness and typicality, at once folksy and abstract, like a Quaker chessboard. A Grocer, a Druggist and Meat confronted a Stationer, a Cafe and Dry-Cleaning; beyond these emblems of a community, trees and a steeple, admonishing, Italianate, of limestone capped with lead; then cirrus, and then blue sky.

The taxi stand was empty.

He carried his suitcases past the Stationer (whose windows celebrated the novels of B. S. Johnson and Georgette Heyer, various cookbooks and garden manuals, and Bertrand Russell's autobiography) and to the Cafe, which received him with a lush gust of gaseous grease.

The waitress said, "Ew!"

"Pardon me," he said, "but could you tell me—"

"We had *such* a fire!" She giggled, wiping her full red face with a dirty towel.

"—the name of this town?"

"You wouldn't of believed it. *Nobody* would!"

"Please."

"A cup of tea?" She drew tea from the steaming urn, set the cup before him. "There's milk." In a stainless steel pitcher. "And there's sugar." In a glass bowl.

She wiped the towel across the plastic joke that hung above the low entrance to the kitchen: YOU DON'T HAVE TO BE CRAZY TO WORK HERE–BUT IT HELPS! She glanced back to see whether he had noticed, whether he would laugh.

"Could you *tell me* the name of this town? Please."

"Village you mean." Pouting, she gave the plastic another swipe.

"Very well, the name of this village."

"Because towns are bigger. I don't care for towns, myself. They're impersonal. People forget that you're a human being. And we're *all* human beings, you know. Do you want toast?"

"No, thank you. If you—"

"Negg?"

"No. I—"

"You don't look like you've had breakfast."

"I'm afraid I got off the train by mistake. That's why I asked the name of this village. It does have a name, doesn't it?"

"You must take me for some kind of simpleton, Mister. I suppose next you'll want to know what year it is? And then maybe how many shillings in a pound?" New billows of grease blossomed from the doorway behind her. "Oh, the hell with it!" she shouted. She ran into the kitchen to swat at the burning griddle with her towel.

He left sixpence on the corner, for his tea, and went back outside. A tiny taxi was waiting at the taxi stand. The driver waved his plaid cap. "Hi there!"

A short man, blond and ruddy, a Scandinavian in miniature. He took the suitcases and swung them on to his luggage rack.

"Looks like you've had quite a night," he observed. His face suggested, but did not assert, bland strength and muscle contentment.

"Could be."

The driver opened the back door. His smile metered a precise quantity of bonhomie. "Hop in."

A cardboard sign was taped to the glass partition between the halves of the taxi. DRIVE CAREFULLY. THE LIFE YOU LEAD MAY BE YOUR OWN.

"What a beautiful morning, eh?" He had taken his place behind the steering wheel, on the left side of the car. "Where to? Are you going to pay the penalty?"

"How's that?"

"For last night, the penalty for last night." (Wink.) "Or will it be a hair of the dog?"

"Actually, I thought we might drive to the next town."

"Which?"

"What *is* the next town?"

"This is just a local service, you know. But I could take you to the beach."

"Take me to the police."

"Don't take offense, mister. Can't a fellow make a joke?"

"It has nothing to do with you. I simply want to ask them a few questions."

"You're the boss."

They drove, on the right side of the road, past Grocer,

Druggist and Meat. There the concrete, encountering green grass, split in two and they took the ONE WAY left, between an ornamental, unpopulated park and coy, numbered cottages of gingerbread and vanilla fudge, wee nightmares of inexorable charm.

"Tell me," he said, in a tone of cautious indifference, "how do you *pronounce* the name of this town?"

The driver scratched his head. "Well, you know . . . it isn't really big enough to be called a *town*."

"More of a village, I suppose you'd say."

The driver, without slowing, turned around. A big, big smile. "You took the words out of my mouth."

He settled back into the plasticine and gave the streets of the Village the same serious attention one must give to a sore tooth. In the park quincunxes of clipped trees alternated with beds of late drooping tulips and fresh poppies. The residences that looked across to this allegory of dullness tried to compensate for its civic stolidity with a kind of metronomic whimsy, as though in each of these die-stamped witch's cottages there lived a banker in a party hat. Chance and individual enterprise could not, unassisted, have created an atmosphere so uniformly oppressive; this village was the conception, surely, of a single, and slightly monstrous, mind, some sinister Disney set loose upon the world of daily life.

The question was—had this vast stage set been inhabited yet? Where were the elves and gnomes and fairies, the village maidens and the village youths, the old old women in white linen wimples and bombazeen skirts, the old men sucking the enormous pipes on which they had carved their own grotesque and wrinkled effigies? For the little taxi had not passed by another vehicle, and the pavements on the left were as empty as the gravel paths on the right. He had seen, at a distance, a single gardener, crawling through a tulip bed. There had been, moreover, the waitress, and there was now this taxi driver, but neither of them seemed large enough, somehow, for the great godawfulness of the Place. They were not much better than toy soldiers four inches tall while the set demanded figures at least half life-size.

The park eventually grew bored with itself, at which point a church had grown up in the middle of the road. It almost seemed real.

He said, "Stop." It stopped.

He got out. He walked toward the church. He mounted the first, the second, the third step. There were many, many more and then a door.

"Cremona?" he wondered.

No, not Cremona. Somewhere else.

"Bergamo?"

Not Bergamo either. But *someplace*, certainly.

"Now that *is* a pretty church." The miniature taxi driver had come out of his miniature taxi. His approval encompassed church, park, the beautiful morning, the universe, without, for all that, coming right out in favor of anything. It was possible, after all, that it was *not* a pretty church. What do taxi drivers know about churches?

"You religious?" he asked.

Was he religious?

"I was thinking," he said (it was not an answer, but then what answers had *he* got this morning?) "that I've been here before."

"Lots of people get that feeling. Here."

"In front of the church?"

"In the Village, generally. It seems to do that. You know what I think it is?"

"What?"

"I think it *represents* something." He stroked his small, square chin, savoring the plum of *represents*. "People come here from other places. Like you. And they see our Village, and they get the feeling that something has always been *missing* from their lives."

"And the Village represents that, the thing that is missing from their lives?"

"It was only my idea," the taxi driver demurred. Clearly, it was doubtful whether taxi drivers ought to have ideas.

"And this thing that's missing–what is it?"

Startled, the taxi driver looked for it on the steps, up in the steeple, admonishing, Italianate, in the cirrus clouds.

"Something good? Or–"

"Oh, certainly! Something like . . . I don't know . . ." He turned to his taxi for help. "Like being contented!" Triumphantly.

"With?"

"With?"

"What is it like being contented with?"

The taxi driver shrugged. "This kind of life. The kind of life that the Village represents."

"The way it contents *you*?"

"Oh my god! Jesus! Of course! Say, what is this? Where are you going?"

"Don't you remember? To the police."

"Yeah. Well then, let's go there."

The police station (it lay not more than fifty yards from the church) occupied the gray stone building that would have been, in the usual scheme of things, the episcopal residence. A mansard roof peered out over the top of adolescent elms, each one protected from the world by its own individualized prison of wrought-iron spikes that dissembled their ferocity as fleurs-de-lis.

He approached the door (it was the kind of door that insists upon ceremony, like a rich relative who had only condescended to visit this house after many misgivings) slowly, gravely, as though he might shame some kind of justice out of this Village by his own stern gaze and conscious dignity.

He pushed the bronze handle of the door. He pulled.

He read the card in the small glass frame above the bell. Its brief message was printed in florid script, like a wedding invitation:

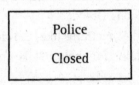

Police

Closed

With a wonderful sense of appropriateness, the taxi driver chose just that moment to make his break for it. He had left the two Knocabouts on the curb.

He walked through a bed of marigolds to stand beneath the window just left of the door. He looked into what appeared to be the waiting room of a very fashionable dentist. The armchairs were decorated with antimacassars of yellowed lace, the end tables with copies of *Vogue* and *Bazaar*. A framed document (the dentist's diploma?) punctuated the rhythm, mild as Mantovani, of the wallpaper. The room was empty.

He walked, with less mercy now for marigolds, to the

next window. This was the dentist's office, where, at a Danish teakwood desk, his stenographer took dictation in the morning, where, twice a week, his cleaning lady dusted the shelves, where it was demonstrated to clients that there was no need to be afraid, it wouldn't hurt at all.

At all the other windows, the blinds were drawn and the curtains lowered. There was no way to know therefore, whether things went quite as smoothly for the dentist's patients as they had been led to hope. Probably he used gas. Or might it be that he had taken such good care of *everyone's* teeth that he had simply put himself out of business?

Abandoning the marigolds to a lingering death he returned to his bags. Fortunately Hartmann luggage is designed for people who have no patience with porters: his hands gripped the moulded leather as naturally as though he had picked up a pair of perfectly mated foils. He took his way west along a residential street that promised to take him more directly than the boulevard bounding the park back to the railway office.

He had not quite lost sight of the police station before he saw it ahead on the left, set back only a few feet from the pavement: his new home, the converted gatehouse he had leased through Chandler & Carr. There, at the corner of the steep tile roof, was the glided weathercock he had intended to take down as his first act of possession. There was that single dormer window, standing open now as it had stood open in all the photographs, like certain celebrated politicians who can command, during an entire career, only a single facial expression, which they wear, like a badge of office, to every function they attend. There (he stood directly before the gatehouse now) was the big red number torn living from a first-form workbook for arithmetic and screwed to the oak muntin of the door:

6

And there, with his hand resting on it, was the brass knob of that door.

The hand and the knob rotated clockwise ninety degrees. The door swung open.

The furniture that he might have bought (could he have afforded it) yesterday in London–the chairs he had seen at Mallett's, the table from J. Cornelius, the Sirhaz carpet, the Riesener secretaire, even the three-legged, spiraling object that had amused him momentarily by its studious lack of any other purpose than that of standing, as now, upright against a wall–was disposed about the room, his living room, just as he might himself have disposed it. It was as though the usual gap between desire and necessity had been bridged during some freakish fit to absent-mindedness on the part of old Father Reality, temporarily indisposed with sunspots. His first sensation could not be anything except pleasure, for here were all his pumpkins turned into carriages with the gilt still fresh and the price tags in full view. But if one is not willing to believe in fairy godmothers, such pleasures burst at a finger's touch: they are not real.

What then, with any certainty, was?

He thought he recognized the answer in a mirror, until he noticed with chagrin, that his trouser-fly had been left unbuttoned.

By himself?

No. Though he *seemed* to remember, now, forgetting to do this.

The Village, this splendid room, the mirror in its frame of ormolu, and even the image in the mirror were not to be trusted. What, then, was?

His body, the body beneath these wrinkled evening clothes, that could be trusted.

And his mind.

Because these things could not be tampered with.

He could trust (as finally, we all must) himself.

Chapter Four

The Villagers

"Can I help you?" a woman's voice asked.

"Please. I am trying to reach a number in London-COVentry-6121."

"I'm sorry, there is no provision for me to accept long distance calls from a public telephone."

"And *I'm* sorry, but this is an urgent call. I have no telephone at my residence. I'm sure the party who answers will accept the charges."

"I'm sorry, there is no provision—"

"Then let me speak to your supervisor."

A click, a hum, two clicks, and a muted rattle. Then she said: "COVentry-6121?"

"Yes."

"I will see if there is a line free." Then, after a suitable interval: "I am sorry, but at present our outside lines are all engaged. If you would like to wait, I will call back as soon as—"

"I'll try and place the call later; thank you."

He left the glass booth, and the man with goitres who had been fretting outside the door all this while rushed in and began to speak excitedly into the telephone in a language that resembled Bulgarian. He had not bothered to dial.

He returned to his seat on the flagstone terrace, at the table farthest from the chirruping little orchestra. He looked out to the sea where, a brighter white amid the whiteness of the midday haze, a sailboat came about and made toward the northern limit of the bay. He took a small cigar from his leather case and lighted it, shielding the match against a salt breeze that puttered aimlessly about the terrace, fluttering the fringes of umbrellas, the pages of menus, the hems of skirts, moving now in from the sea and then a moment later moving out toward it, fitful as a child with nothing he can do and no one he can play with.

The waitress returned to his table and asked, in a voice as crisp as the black nylon of her uniform whether he had made up his mind.

"Coffee."

"Just coffee? Wouldn't you like to see the pastry cart?"

"No, just coffee."

"A sandwich perhaps?"

"Very well, a roast beef sandwich."

She shook her head. "We don't *do* roast beef, sir. When you've made up your mind, I'll come back." She remained standing by his table, looking westward to the obscured horizon. Her hand brushed a gauze of blond hair from her eyes.

"It's a remarkable view," he said, "from up here."

"Yes, it must be. Everyone says so. And some days it's much better than this. You can see all the way out there."

"You must become quite busy here, this time of year."

"Never much busier than this, really, and never much quieter either."

"But the tourists . . . ?"

"Oh, tourists never find their way *here*. You're not a tourist, are you?"

"More or less. Unless, just by being here, I'm not."

She smiled morosely. "That's rather good–I'll have to remember that. But I'd better get your coffee now. And I'll see if we have any roast beef left." She hurried off toward the small brick building behind the platform where the orchestra of three old men was wending its weary way through Ziehrer's *Faschingskinder Waltz*.

A sparrow hopped from the flagstones up to the rough ledge of the escarpment, paused to estimate the drop, and flung itself over the edge. A moment later it was back, as though, even for sparrows, there were no passage down to that empty beach.

He watched the sea with the patience of a carved face staring out from a sandstone cliff. It was not that he lacked a plan of action. He had known from the moment of waking that he ought to depart this Village by any means available. If he lingered, it was a sign only that he did not yet doubt that means of some sort were available. He would leave whenever he determined to leave, but meanwhile each new increment of fact made him hungrier for the synthesis that would make of the scattered pieces a coherent picture. He had every reason to expect to dislike that picture, but he did want to *see* it.

That he was himself intended to form an element of that picture he could no more doubt than that the clothes he wore–the slacks, the turtleneck, the jacket fraying at its cuffs–had been tailored for just his frame and no other.

But when, exactly, had they (omitting the question of who "they" were) recruited *him* in their conspiracy against himself? Had he already been, in a sense, cooperating with them at the moment he had chosen to lease just that particular converted gatehouse in Pembroke? It was not a facsimile–he had assured himself of that: it tallied brick for brick and slate for slate with the photographs. As it was simpler to suppose that he had been *led* somehow to elect this choice than that the whole elaborate absurdity of the Village had been constructed suddenly about some building he had simply chanced to like, it followed that he had been tampered with, like a clock that has been set back to provide the murderer with a false alibi.

But if his choice had been less free than it had seemed, *how* had it been coerced? A question that was posed, more subtly, by the presence of the furniture, furniture that he had only, and in the idlest manner possible, *wished* for.

And what (this question, which concluded the series, had occurred to him within moments of entering the house) were they expecting of him now? Would not the first, the most natural reaction have been to run away? But he was not–and they must know this–likely to react with such Pavlovian simplicity.

And so, while he weighed this imponderable against that and pursued each question till it vanished into paradox, he had temporised. He had unpacked his suitcases and disposed their effects into closets and drawers, convinced, as he did so, that whatever they were expecting from him it would not be that. He had inspected the kitchen (the icebox was well stocked, and he helped himself to a lager and some cheddar cheese) and then the other rooms of the ground floor. He determined that there was no staircase leading to the floor above, either within or without, though there was space between his ceiling and the eaves for a suite of rooms not much smaller than his own. He attempted to enter the upper floor through the open dormer window and discovered, without surprise, a second wall, just behind the window, of solid iron-plate. He dug out from his watch pocket the house-key Mr Chandler had handed him in ratification of the lease; there was no lock on any door to which this, or any, key might be fitted. He looked for a telephone and found none. He showered and changed into fresh clothes. He made himself at home.

It was not yet noon when he left the house, returning the way he'd come, past the retired police station, past the steps of the church, from which vantage he had seen the elephantine umbrellas of the terrace restaurant. There, though he were visible to them, *they* would become much less invisible to him. He could not imagine grounds for any greater uncertainty than these on which he stood, in which he sank, and so, on the theory that he could only get out of their hands by playing into them, he let himself be led to the reserved table.

As soon as the man with goitres left her, the tweedy woman in the Tyrolean hat gestured more emphatically for his attention. She was fiftyish, tailored, and stout in an agreeable, oaken way. Her hair was shingled and her face so carefully made up as to seem almost her own. Having caught his eye, she gave him a long, apparently significant, yet incomprehensible look. She rooted in the bottom of a swollen canvas satchel, not quite a purse and not quite a shopping bag, and with the stub of pencil she exhumed she began scribbling on a paper napkin. She had finished before the goitres came back.

Humoresque fell dying to the flagstones, and the elderly violinist bowed low in acknowledgment of his defeat. Raindrops of applause spattered the terrace. The tweedy woman lifted her pigskin fingers to pantomime her mildest approval, and the breeze whisked up the paper napkin thereby released and harried it from table to table until it lodged beside the metal leg of that adjoining his.

The clarinet hobbled into the *Swedish Rhapsody.* He stooped forward to retrieve the napkin, but the man with goitres had preceded him by an instant: "Allow *me*, please." He put the napkin in his pocket.

"That was very thoughtful of the gentleman," said the tweedy woman, who had followed the goitres to his table.

"And very careless of you, my dear. You must excuse my wife."

"It was no inconvenience."

The goitres quivered.

"None at all."

"You see, it was a sort of . . . sketch . . . a map I drew in order to explain to my husband—" A pigskin glove caught hold of the man's arm, so that there should be no doubt who was meant: this was her husband, *this*. "—just how . . . the Prater is laid out. Have you been to the Prater, may I ask?"

"Yes, though not recently."

"Didn't I tell you, my dear, that he looked like a man

who has traveled? I have always admired travelers. Travel is a kind of passion with me, but, alas . . ."

"Alas," her husband continued for her, "my wife's health does not permit her to travel."

She nodded. "My health does not permit me to travel."

They glared at one another, each stonily determined not to be the first to depart.

"Won't you share my table?" he suggested. "I'll have the waitress bring more coffee."

The woman thumped into a chair. "Thank you. We always enjoy—"

"My wife," the goitres announced, livid with courtesy, "does not—"

"—seeing a strange face. *Don't* we?"

"—*drink* coffee. The doctor forbids it."

She stared up at him. "So we must ask him to be kind enough to order lemonade for me!"

He seated himself, with ill grace, on the edge of the metal chair, which he did not trouble to draw toward the table.

"Perhaps now you can tell us," she said, rising to the alto register, "something about Vienna. Do you love the Opera?"

"I would have thought, actually, that you could tell me much more about Vienna than I could tell you."

Her laughter, mirthless and operatic, disrupted the gambols of the breathless clarinet. "Would you listen to him, my dear! He thinks that I . . . that *I* . . ."

"My wife," the goiters explained sullenly, "has never left this Village. Due to her unfortunate health."

"But surely before she came here . . . ?"

The clarinet resumed its rhapsody. The woman placed

an expressive glove upon her tweed bosom. "I was *born* in this Village. Alas."

"Really."

"Do you find that surprising?"

"Yes, in one who has such a passion for traveling. Or unfortunate, to say the least."

"Passions are stronger for being unrequited," the goitres remarked, with evident satisfaction. He even edged his chair some inches nearer.

She leaned forward intently until the feather in her cap was brushing his chin. "Have you been, as well, to Italy?"

The goiters stiffened. "Really, my dear!"

"If my questions offend him, he needn't answer, you know."

"What offense is there in asking that? Yes, I've seen quite a lot of Italy."

"Venice," she muttered balefully. "Florence. Rome."

"And to a number of the smaller towns. I'm very fond of Bergamo."

"Bergamo! Where they make those wonderful violins?"

"You're thinking of Cremona, my dear."

"Cremona, of course. We'll he's probably been there too. I read about Cremona in *The National Geographic*. Do you know that magazine? It's been the chief comfort of my life, excepting, needless to say, my husband. In fact, I am a Member of the Society!"

"You *used* to be," her husband amended.

"I used to be, yes."

"I'm afraid the waitress has gone into hiding," the goitres said, rising to his feet. "I shall have to go and seek her out."

When he was out of earshot, the tweedy woman caught hold of his hand. Despite her agitation, her grip seemed weak, almost languid. "You heard all of that!"

"Yes, but I'm afraid I understood very little."

"Isn't it clear? Isn't it obvious? *I am a prisoner!* They never let me out of their sight."

"Then what your husband said about your health . . ."

"Oh, him! He's one of them, you know. He helps them every way he can. Not that it makes a speck of difference to *them*! That's why I tried to give you that message–to warn you!"

"I'm afraid I still don't–"

"Oh good heavens, man–don't you see? It's staring you in the face. If *you* don't see it, then you're the only one here who doesn't."

"That I'm a prisoner, too, you mean?"

"Of course."

He shook his head.

She backed away. "Then . . . you are one of them!"

"I am neither."

She stood up, clutching her canvas bag to her stomach. "My husband is waiting for me. We're expected somewhere else. I'm sorry to have *disturbed* you."

"You needn't apologize. On the contrary, I owe you my thanks for your confidence. And for trying to help."

Her lips wavered between scorn and commiseration. Her eyes tried to meet his, but always it was the man with goitres fidgeting on the other side of the terrace who commanded her attention.

"So that's what it was I was trying to do, eh?"

"Weren't you? It's what you said."

Commiseration won out. "There you have it! That's just

the special horror of this place–that you never *can* decide, when someone offers to help, what it is they have in mind. I would love to stay and talk, dear boy, but look at my husband–he's getting ready to murder me."

She patted his hand. *"Wiederseh'n."*

"Goodbye."

"Hello?" He jiggled the hook. "Hello?"

Silence displaced the vague static; dead silence.

"This is the operator. Can I help you?"

"The number I've been trying to reach in London–it rang twice and there seemed to be an answer. And then the line went dead."

"Would you like me to try that number again?"

"If you would. COVentry-6121."

The operator performed veiled mysteries at her switchboard, and once again the receiver echoed a hopeful Bizz, Zim; a second; a third, still hopefully, and then:

"Hello?" A woman's voice.

"Hello, Liora?"

"This is Better Books. May I help you?"

"Is this COVentry-6121?"

A pause. "Well, almost. It's COVent Garden-6121. Same letters. Did you want Better Books?"

"No, but perhaps you *can* help me. I'm outside London, and I've had considerable difficulty getting through to that number. I know it exists. I reached someone there only yesterday. Do you have a London Directory on hand?"

"Somewhere."

"Would you look at the front, where the exchanges are listed, and find COVentry? Perhaps it's not among the central London exchanges."

"Is this some kind of a joke? Who is this?"

"Believe me, I'm perfectly serious. I wouldn't put you to the trouble if I could receive any kind of cooperation from the operators here."

"Well, just a second."

In fact, a minute forty-five seconds.

"I find no COVentry exchange. Just COVent Garden. It makes sense, doesn't it? They wouldn't have two exchanges with the same letters?"

"You looke down both lists? Central and Suburban?"

"Yes of course. Say, is this Lee Harwood?"

"No, I don't think so. Well, thank you. I'm sorry to put you to any trouble."

Better Books made a doubtful sound and hung up.

He stared for a while, with the receiver still in his hand, at the telephone dial. He replaced the receiver on its hook and stepped out of the booth.

He found himself looking directly into the kitchen that served the terrace restaurant. There, sitting on the chopping block beside a monumental double-sink, was the blond waitress who had served him on the terrace. She was bent double, her knees pulled up to hide her face. The nylon uniform was bunched into her lap, exposing the sallow flesh of her thighs. Her sobbing followed the slow tiddle-tiddle-thump of the distant orchestra.

He stepped across the threshold on to slippery, garbage-strewn concrete. "What is it?" he asked quietly.

Fear glistened in the smudged eyes. Her mouth gaped, and clenched. Hands tugged the nylon down to her knees.

"Is there some way I can help?"

A small noise rose from her chest, strangled in her

convulsing throat, as though at some far distance her twin had screamed and her own body had taken up, this faintly, the resonance.

"Go away," she whispered. "Leave me! Oh, leave me, leave this town. Why did you—Oh, stop *looking* at me, for God's sake, stop!"

Chapter Five

Something White

The old woman standing by the greeting card rack satisfied, better than anyone he had seen yet, his ideal conception of what a resident of this village ought to look like. The wispy white hair caught up in a bun, the silverpoint wrinkles, the knobby, venerable hands, the stooped shoulders and fallen bosom, the crepe falling in black folds to her ankles, allowing just a glimpse of what might even be button shoes: she was in herself a more perfect greeting card than any of those that, with many a low chuckle and many a nod and a smile, she read aloud to herself in a dry, slow, delighted drone.

The clerk, a middle-aged gentleman suitably dressed for a dinner party in Surbiton, appeared from beneath the counter. He held a feather duster rigidly in one hand, an allegory of his trade. "Can I—" His courtesy exploded into coughing; he covered his mouth discreetly with the feather duster, sneezed, sniffed.

"I'd like a newspaper," he said. "Any newspaper for today."

The clerk blinked back tears. "I'm so sorry." He touched the knot in his tie, the handkerchief in his breast pocket, trying, by as much as it lay in *his* power, to make this a better world. "You see, we don't . . ." He laughed self-deprecatingly. "You understand, surely, that it isn't me . . ."

"You're trying to tell me that you don't handle newspapers."

The clerk sighed. "Just so—we don't handle them."

"I wanted something to read on the train."

"On the . . . ? Yes, well! That's . . . There's . . ." He stabbed the air with the duster. ". . . lots of books. Do you like to read . . . books?"

"I'd prefer a magazine."

"Oh yes, magazines, those, yes. We keep the magazines over in that corner: *Country Life*. And *Hair-Do*, but no, you wouldn't . . . *Car and Driver*? *Analog*? Or that one there, on the top, with the greenish cover and that lovely what is it, some kind of, oh, that's for children, isn't it? *Muscular Development*, mm? If you could give me . . . some idea?"

"I'd like a *New Statesman*."

"No, I don't think . . . We don't receive much *demand*, you see, for—"

"*The Spectator*? *Newsweek*?"

"Not that sort of thing, really. That's all, how would you say, politics, isn't it? They say there's two things you should never discuss—politics and religion."

"Then perhaps you could tell me, at least, when the train departs?"

"Which train?"

"Any at all. Preferably one this afternoon. I've been to

the station twice today. The ticket window is always closed, and no schedules are posted."

"Yes. Well. I think they're on the *summer* schedule now. But I'm not at all sure. If you asked at the station . . ."

"I've just come from the station. There was no one there."

"Did you look around? They might have been somewhere else, you know, doing something."

"Where do you suggest I look?"

"Oh . . . Oh, that's difficult. I'm not really qualified, am I? I mean, this is just a *book* store. People don't buy their train tickets at book stores, now do they? So unless there's something that . . . ? You can see for yourself that there *are* other customers."

They both looked at the other customer, who glanced sideways at them, smiling, and jiggled an embossed and glittering birthday card, enticing them to share its message with her.

"Thank you for your help."

"Not at all. Think nothing of it. I try to do what I . . ." And, his eyes seemed to express, if that wasn't very much, it wasn't *his* fault.

The sweeper, a thick suet pudding of a fellow, tackled his job with great zeal, conscientiously oblivious to the fact that his broom, this third time around, raised no dust, none, from the floorboards. It was his job to sweep, and so he swept on. Perhaps he was motivated less by a conception of duty than by an admiration for the tools of his craft. It was a wide and quite handsome broom, in perfect condition, the bristles still fresh, soft, and supple. No one could ask for a better broom than this. His uniform was no less handsome, of heavy black twill on which had been lavished all manner of pleats, pockets, buckles, zippers, snaps, and, on the back, in chartreuse script, the insignia *Department of Sanitation*. He was equipped, in addition, with a fine leather harness (black) that suggested immense utility, though, unless he were to be harnessed to a plow, it was hard to imagine any real use for it.

The broom bumped his shoe. The sweeper, encountering this unprecedented obstruction, stopped. The sweeper, temporarily deactivated, considered this obstruction and how best to deal with it.

The sweeper spoke. He said: "Hey! You. What are you doing here?"

"I'm waiting for a train."

"Huh? What train?"

"This is a railway waiting room. Outside there are tracks for trains. I arrived here this morning by train, and I'm waiting now for another in order to leave."

"Uh. But. It's closed."

"In that case how is it that the door is standing open?"

The sweeper looked at the open door. He looked at his broom. He looked at the face of the clock. The big hand was on XI; the little hand was on IV. He tapped the clock with a thick, segmented sausage of finger. He said: "Look at the time."

"I've been looking at it for hours. Perhaps you can tell me when the next train leaves?" A very far-out possibility, but he would mention it.

"Uh. You ask the ticket window man about that. I just sweep."

"There is no ticket window man to ask."

"That's because we're closed." It followed logically, it did!

"Since the waiting room is closed, I'll wait outside on the platform."

Which he did.

In a few moments the sweeper had followed him out the door, trailing his fine broom in dejection. "Hey. You. It's closed."

"How can it be closed when there are still people waiting for a train?"

The sweeper stood on his two feet and confronted this question, as though it had been a wall erected just in front of him in the middle of the platform.

"Well. Anyhow." (Climbing over the wall.) "You can't sit there. I got to sweep."

He stood up. The sweeper swept. From the other end of the platform a third figure approached them. The sweeper stopped sweeping. He smiled. "You talk to him. Okay?"

The approaching figure was of the secular (as opposed to the official, and uniformed) order, a prodigy of good grooming, good taste, and good cheer. As a model he would have commanded the very highest rates: well-built but not *so* well-built that you could not imagine those same clothes looking almost as nice on you; bright, even teeth (his grin broadened as he grew nearer) that would have done credit to any toothpaste; a prominent bone structure that one might photograph from any angle. He could have worn the most implausible clothing and yet it would have seemed, on him, fashionable rather than peculiar. He approached, grinning, within three feet, within two, and then, with as much grace as efficiency, he swung his fist into the stomach of the man who had begun to ask, once more, about the trains.

Who was answered, as well, by the handle of the broom in the small of his back. Vertebrae crunched.

He doubled up.

Caught hold of the manicured hand chopping at his neck. Twisted, left, twisted, farther left. The buckled, square-toed shoes slipped.

The bristly end of the broom swept on a long arc toward that point in space his head had occupied only a second before; which now was occupied by the more photogenic head of the model.

The handle of the broom broke off at its base.

He had stopped. Now, taking leverage on the suddenly limp wrist, he lifted the well-built body up: up higher. And dumped it into the suet pudding. A buckle-shoe caught in the harness. The harness gave.

The sweeper looked unhappily at the body littering the platform. "You shouldn't," he said, in a tone more of disappointment than of disapproval.

"Neither, for that matter, should you."

He hit the sweeper in the stomach.

He hit the sweeper in the stomach a second time.

He hit the sweeper in the stomach a third time.

The sweeper lifted his arms in self-defense.

Sometimes his fists sank into the pudding, sometimes they were deflected. The sweeper stepped over the pile of litter. Grabbed for a blue lapel with white piping.

His fists battered at the blinking face. Seams strained, split. The sweeper got a better grip, beneath the swinging arms. He lifted, tightening his hold, oblivious, as a bear to bee stings, to the pelting hands, the kicking feet; hugging, more tightly still, the small of that back.

Thinking: *Break, godammit, break!*

Then:

(The sweeper did not understand this, but he didn't let it distract him.)

They were on the platform, the other body tangled beneath their legs. They rolled, in each other's grasp, across the well-swept boards. The sweeper's head bumped the frame of the door. They rolled back. His head bumped the frame of the door, again. They rolled into the waiting room. His hands and arms and head concentrated on squeezing the small of that back.

He began to choke.

Eventually, his attention was distracted by this choking. The man he grasped was not hitting him any longer. Instead he was pulling at the broken straps of the harness. The straps were across his neck.

He understood everything now: the man was choking him with the harness straps.

He relaxed his hold to grab for . . .

To get . . .

But the straps were embedded too deeply in his flesh. Too tightly. He could not get . . .

He choked.

His head stopped thinking. His arms flopped.

He stood above the sweeper, listened to the wheeze from his welted throat. His own breath came irregularly. He looked at himself in the mirror of the gum machine. The left lapel had been torn from his coat. He removed his bill-fold from the breast pocket, dropped the coat in a wire basket, Property of the Village.

The movement of the sweeper's arms indicated his

return to consciousness. He put his shoulder against the back of the gum machine and shoved. The machine crashed down on the sweeper, whose arms once more relaxed.

The body outside was still quiet.

He jumped from the platform down to the track and began walking east along the ties. He stopped at intervals to remove a cinder from his shoe, but on the whole he made good time.

He passed no houses. The station had been built at the easternmost limit of the Village. The track stretched on across a perfectly even and featureless plain, and so it was some time before he was out of sight of the station. A mile away Nature grew bolder and asserted herself with, here and there, a shrub of dogwood or a spindle tree. Saxifrage, iridescent as puddles of oil, squinted out from the cinder bed. Dandelions bred promiscuously amid the select gatherings of their betters–knapweed, butterbur and sneezewort yarrow.

There were no birds. There was nothing in all this landscape, except himself, that moved or made noises.

Two miles from the Village the tracks stopped, abruptly. The meadow continued, without the aid of perpective lines, to the horizon.

A white sphere stood at the horizon, or just before it. Its size could not be estimated with any exactness. Twelve feet? Fifteen feet? More?

The sphere approached, rolling smoothly and easily across the weeds, westward, away from its shadow.

He broke into a run.

The sphere swerved right, its silhouette warping momentarily with the torsion: it was soft.

It was very big.

He crouched, shielding his head in his arms. The sphere slammed into him, knocking him off his knees. He slid on his side several feet through the weeds. The sphere bounced high into the air, settled gelatinously, bounced, settled, quivered.

He stood up, nursing his right shoulder, which had taken the brunt of the collision. The sphere edged toward him, nudged; pushed. He pushed back at the yielding white skin, but the great bulk of it moved on, resistless as a bulldozer. He slithered, braced against the advancing sphere, across a mulch of crushed weeds and meadowgrass, until, his heel catching in soft earth, he could not slide. The straining muscles accordioned, he collapsed. The sphere moved back.

He stood, wincing at the pain. An ankle sprained. The sphere rolled forward, nudged. He stepped back. The sphere stopped. He walked slowly backward, facing the sphere.

He began angling to his left, still moving backward. The sphere, like an anxious collie, corrected his false trajectory.

He angled to the right, which the sphere permitted until he had returned to the tracks. Thereafter no deviation from the true path was allowed. The sphere insisted that he return to the station. It insisted that he walk along, between the rails, at a moderate pace, back to the Village. It did allow him to stop at intervals to remove a cinder from his shoe, but it would not tolerate indolence on any larger scale.

Chapter Six

Something Blue

A shrill voice, but when it broke, which occurred at almost every point of emphasis, it became, quite evidently, a man's. When it was most strident it seemed to possess overtones beyond the range of human audibility, pitched, perhaps, for dogs or bats, It spoke:

"You!

"Number 6!

"Pay attention please." The clearing of . . . a throat? a microphone? "I am addressing *you*. Will you stop fussing over that pot and come into the living room?"

He placed the artichoke on the wire rack above the boiling water, placed the lid on the pot, set the timer at thirty-five minutes. Sliced the roll, set its halves beneath the broiler to toast. Folded his arms.

"I'm waiting. This obstinacy can only make matters more difficult for you, you know. For my own part, there are many other things I can do besides watching this cooking lesson. Are you listening to me, Number 6?

"Number 6?"

"My name is not Number 6. So, if it is me that you address, you would do well to use my name. If you don't know it, which I doubt, you might introduce yourself. Then, perhaps, I'll do as much for you."

"Oh, fuss and bother. *I* am Number 2. For administrative purposes, numbers are much more convenient than names, and more reasonable as well. In this Village there might be any number of people with the same first name as you, or, in your case, even the same surname. But there can only be *one* Number 6, Number 6."

"And only one Number 2?"

"Precisely. Numbers have the further advantage that they are meaningful. When I say that I am Number 2, that you are Number 6, that tells us something about our relationship. *Will* you stop buttering that roll and come into the living room?"

"I'd spoil my supper if I left off now. And in any case, I'd prefer to speak to Number 1. You may tell him that."

"For you even to suggest that shows how little you understand your position–or mine. I have full authority to handle your case, rest assured. What are you making there?"

He took the roll, brown crust bubbling with butter, turned the oven to a low heat, placed it inside to dry. Poured the egg yolks into the top of the double broiler: they swirled into the melted butter.

"Eggs Beaugency. This is the sauce."

"Well, leave it."

"Leave a Béarnaise sauce? You must be insane."

"You don't seem to realize your position here, Number 6. If you did, you wouldn't jeopardize those advantages you possess—such as my readiness to indulge you in this fantasy that you are free to oppose me."

"It's an uncomfortable position. And I intend to change it."

"You are a prisoner, Number 6. It is as simple as that."

"I doubt that even in this Village anything is as simple as that. I am not Number 6. I am not a prisoner. I am a free man."

"Ah, philosophy! I cherish philosophy, but of course in *your* situation it becomes downright necessary. There was a philosopher of ancient Rome, Horace (no doubt you've heard of him), who wrote: 'Who, then is free? The wise man who can govern himself.' Now that's philosophy all over!"

"More to the point, he said: *Hic murus aeneus esto, nil conscire sibi, nulla pallescere culpa.*"

"Don't your English public schools do wonderful things? There was never time, the way things went for me, to learn a classical language. I've always been kept going up and down, to and fro, *doing* things."

"You're American?"

"My accent? It's mid-Atlantic, actually. And in other ways, Number 6, you'll discover that I'm not *quite* what I seem." A chuckle.

Then: "It must be a burden for you, Number 6, to stand there stirring that Béarnaise sauce, when there must be so many questions that you want to ask."

"Not so difficult when my questions produce no answers."

"Always these suspicions, Number 6! Always this hostility, these frowns, this lack of mutuality!

> "If all who hate would love us,
>   And all our loves were true,
> The stars that swing above us,
>   Would brighten in the blue;
> If cruel words were kisses,
>   And every scowl a smile,
> A better world than this is
>   Would hardly be worth while.' "

"Not Horace again, surely?"

"No, an American philosopher–James Newton Matthews. But you meant that as a joke, didn't you? You're feeling a little better. I'm glad to see it. A sense of humor is an absolute necessity in situations like these."

"In prisons?"

"Oh, in general. Once you become accustomed to our life here, you'll find it isn't *that* much different from the world outside. What you might call a microcosm, in fact. We have our local, democratically-elected government."

"It's powers must be rather limited."

"Yes, somewhat. Were it any otherwise, how could I insist on our typicality? Further, our residents enjoy considerable affluence. Your kitchen, for instance–you find it well equipped?"

"It lacks a Mouli and a garlic press, and I don't have much use for tinned spices, unless they're all that's to be had. And for what I'm doing now I should have beef marrow, but that can't be helped."

"I'll make a note of that and speak to Number 84.

Stocking your kitchen was her responsibility, and she'll have cause to regret her carelessness. You see, Number 6, no one is idle here. There is always work to do, and there is always someone to do it. *You* will not be required to take a job, but should you find your leisure becoming a problem—"

"The very least of them."

"A man of your vigor—and without any compulsion to *work*?"

"I am retired, you know."

"So I've been given to understand. And so young too! Thirty-eight?"

"Forty."

"You were born?"

"Yes. On 19 March 1928. Don't you have that in your dossier?"

"You can't expect me to keep track of all of that. You should see your dossier, Number 6—it's very nearly the largest in our files."

"When the eggs are done, I'll take you up on that."

"That sauce isn't ready *yet*? It's rather impersonal to be discussing these matters at such a distance. I distrust a man who won't look me in the eyes."

"Always these suspicions, Number 2! If all who love would hate us, and all our hates were true—"

"You have a point. But as I was saying, about the organization of the Village (forgive me dwelling on a theme so dear to my heart): we also possess excellent recreational facilities. There are clubs that cater to every possible interest: photography, the theater, botany, folk singing. There are discussion groups on comparative religion, on political philosophy (I attend some of those myself), on almost anything that an educated man might want to talk about. We have some lively bridge tournaments, and if you play chess, we can boast three acknowledged masters of the game."

"Have you played against them?"

"Yes, and I've even known to win. Then, what else? Sports? Dear me, all the sportsmen here! We have no less than four elevens. There are soccer teams for both men and women. Tennis is very popular, and squash. Our older citizens amuse themselves at croquet, and the spryer among them badminton. What are your preferences, Number 6?"

"I've always preferred individual sport. But once again, that should be in my dossier."

"Yes, it said that you do quite a bit of boating. Sad to say, no one shows much interest in that here."

"And marksmanship?"

"Oh, Number 6!"

"Boxing, then? I sometimes like to box."

"For shame, Number 6–that *you* should be the one to bring it up! Poor Number 83 is in hospital with concussions. You really didn't have to go that far."

"And the other one?"

"Number 189 is back at his job, sweeping, sweeping. He's quite resilient, that one. But even so, you must recognize how futile these violent outbursts are. Do you think that we'd be so naive as to base our security on a few pairs of fists? Our residents are always under surveillance, and those who are as important to us as you receive individual attention. Whenever you leave your house I'm kept informed of your whereabouts. Should you decide to take a walk into the country–and at this time of year, who can resist to?–you will be brought back to the Village, as you were today, whenever you overstep the boundaries."

"By your big white balls?"

"By a Guardian, yes. Though not all are white. Some are pink. Some are baby blue. A few are mint-green, and there is one–I pray to God that you should never encounter *it*–in fawn."

"And the boundaries, how are they marked?"

"We don't like to deface the natural beauty of the surrounding countryside with unsightly signs and ugly wire fences. If you're curious, you'll discover them soon enough. After all, wasn't it Wordsworth who said–"

'Stone walls do not a prison make nor iron bars a cage.' No, it was Richard Lovelace. In a poem he wrote to his mistress from prison."

"It wasn't Wordsworth? I'm sure he said something, then, to the same effect. Perhaps I'm thinking of:

'This royal throne of kings, this sceptre'd isle,
This earth of majesty, this seat of Mars,
This other Eden, demi-prisonhouse...' "

"Whoever wrote them, they're beautiful lines."

"Stirring, stirring! Well, God bless Richard Lovelace! And how is the sauce Béarnaise coming?"

"You haven't been watching: it's done, and soon the artichoke will be."

"Can't one trust an artichoke to cook itself? Come into the living room a moment and talk seriously, do."

"Very well, but I must have answers then."

"You need only ask the proper questions, Number 6."

He went into the living room.

The damask curtains of the false window framed the smiling image of Number 2. He sat behind a circular blue desk;

behind him, out of focus, hung heavy maroon drapes identical to the real ones framing the screen. Unless his face was naturally blue-gray, the transmitting apparatus could not reproduce flesh tones with any accuracy, though in other respects the image was astonishingly clear.

The camera zoomed in slowly on the face until it occupied the greater part of the window frame; until, from the knobby blue chin to the faint citras-yellow curve (a strand of hair?) bounding the bald blue head, it measured fully four feet. It would have seemed, in other colors than these, a very friendly face. The general spareness of its features–the thin lips, the Draconian nose, the deep-set eyes (were they actually purple?)–could be accounted to age rather than to any sort of meanness. His smile seemed unforced and sincere, and his eyes, despite their dubious color, shared in this good humor.

Fifty years old? Sixty? More?

In short, a nice old man; a bit of a Polonius perhaps, but then Polonius had been a nice old man too.

The four-foot head nodded.

"Now, isn't this much more intimate?"

The voice, imperfectly synchronized with the movement of the lips, lagged a split-second behind the image.

"Why don't you take a chair, Number 6? And we can have ourselves a heart-to-heart talk. Face-to-face. Man-to-man."

"First, my question. It's very simple: what do you want?"

The head showed its profile, as though to make certain that the object inquired after were still there. And turned back, smiling:

"Why, the world, of course. Who is really ever satisfied with less?"

"What do you want *from me*?"

"Information. Only that. Your friendship, though of ines- timable worth, would be almost an embarrassment of riches."

"Go on."

"The information in your head is priceless, Number 6. I don't think you have a proper reckoning of its value."

"Didn't you—"

"Didn't I what?"

He would have to ask this; it was only a matter of time. He took the plunge: "Have I been here before? In this room? In this Village? When you said that just now, it seemed . . ."

"Ah-ha! Now *that* is a most pertinent question. Yes, Number 6, you have been here before. You remember noth- ing of it?"

"I—"

"Such a look, Number 6! Such a look! I've done nothing to deserve that. In fact, I've helped you. I answered your question candidly and truthfully. And I'll go on helping you, if you'll just tell me what other things you want to know."

"How long was I away?"

"Not very long. A month, a year—time is so subjective. May I say, parenthetically, that you seem suddenly much less sure of yourself?"

"I was in London."

"Were you?"

"I remember being there. I remember . . . some things. Other things are vague. And there are areas that are . . . blank."

"Very nicely put, Number 6. That, in a nutshell, is the process of memory. Since I can't very well ask you which things you've forgotten, may I inquire what you do remember?"

"Almost everything that doesn't interest *either* of us very much."

"And that which *would* interest us?"

"Is blank."

"How convenient for you!"

"Am I supposed to believe that this comes to you as a surprise?"

"We suspected that something of the sort had happened. Your behavior today has tended to confirm that."

"And *you* have had no hand in it?"

"In your brainwashing? As a matter of fact, Number 6, no; we haven't. We're not even certain who did. Naturally, your former employers are prime suspects. But on the other hand, all kinds of people *might* have. The information you possess is, as I've said, priceless–and not only to those who, like ourselves, lack it, but equally for those with whom you share it. When you disappeared for your little holiday here, they must have grown quite worried, and when you returned ... Well, put yourself in their place. You seem disgruntled."

"It strikes me that you're being extremely communicative. Which means either that you're lying, or that you have your own nasty reasons for telling the truth."

"The truth in this case is simply so much more interesting than any lie I might invent. I *had* considered suggesting, as an experiment, that you hadn't actually left the Village at all, that your little interlude in London was a hallucination induced in our laboratory. In theory that could have been done. With a competent surgeon and a few drugs, all things are possible. Life, as (I think it was) a *Spanish* philosopher said, is but a dream. Or else he said it's very short, I don't recall. One can make a case for either theory. But why should I want to confuse you more than you must be already? After all, *this* time, Number 6, we have a common cause. We both want to know what it is you've been made to forget–that is, if you *have* forgotten it and aren't just malingering cleverly."

"And if *you* don't already know."

"Well, if we did, then you need have no scruples about confiding in us and letting us help you remember the matter yourself. That would be a very altruistic undertaking."

"Yes. I had already discounted the possibility."

"Splendid. We understand each other now. And we can begin, just as soon as you like, to recover some of that lost time."

"What makes you believe it's still there to be recovered?"

"The fact that you're alive at all. Presumably, you're still considered useful. The surest way to have guaranteed your silence would have been to silence you. And the next surest way, though it would have left you alive, would have–how shall I say?–*reduced* you. The reason that *we* never tampered anymore than we did (though we had *many* opportunities) is because, valuable though your information might prove, you, Number 6, are infinitely more valuable. What price can be set on the autonomy of the individual? Isn't that a fine phrase, by the way–'the autonomy of the individual'? No, that information will still be there: it's just been swept under a rug, so to speak. We need only poke about here and there, peeking under the corners, to find it."

"And who is scheduled to perform this poking and peeking?"

"As Socrates once said, 'Know Thyself.' Or was that Hamlet?"

"You're thinking of 'To thine own self be true.' "

"Ah! 'And it must follow as the night the day, thou canst *then* be false to any man.' How Shakespeare understands the human heart! But to get back: no one but yourself can undertake to dive down into the deeper waters of your head. But we can offer you assistance, someone to handle the pump, as it were. Our Number 14 has helped other people who found themselves in your unfortunate situation."

"By what means?"

"By sympathy! At root it's the *only* means by which one human being can help another. Sympathy in conjunction with some form or other of animal magnetism."

"You'll find that I'm a poor hypnotic subject. I resist."

"Not always, apparently, or you wouldn't be in this bind now. I realized when I brought the matter up that you wouldn't rush into our arms. It's enough for now that you should know they're open."

A bell rang in the kitchen.

A blue finger reached up to pull at a blue ear lobe; the blue smile became a frown of deeper blue. "Now who in hell could that be? They *know* that I'm—"

"It's an artichoke," he said. "You'll have to excuse me. I must poach some eggs."

"By all means. Wasn't it Bismarck who said—"

" 'You can't make an omelette without poaching eggs.' No, it was Jean Valjean."

"Number 6, you'll kill me."

"Not unless you grant me an interview in person, Number 2. Thoughts can't kill."

"And words can never hurt me. Robert Lowell?"

"Jean-Paul Sartre."

He lifted the artichoke gingerly off the rack, poured the sauce in a small pitcher which he placed above the still-steaming water. Selected two eggs, broke them, let them ease into melted butter.

"You do that nicely," the voice said from the living room. Dissociated from the face, it seemed suddenly younger, and at the same time less benevolent. "If you're serious about establishing a more personal relationship, perhaps I can invite myself to dinner. This Friday, say?"

"Sorry. My engagement calendar is filled for months ahead. I lead a full life."

"It does say in your dossier that you're hard to get to know. But I've always held that it's just such people who end up being most worth knowing."

"That's too bad. I feel I know *you* very well already."

"You're depressed, that's why you're like this. It's still your first day back at home, and it's been a busy, busy day. And then, finding out on top of everything else that someone's been diddling with your head, that's the kicker, that's the unkindest cut of all. You must try to remember the positive aspects of your situation, however."

"I'll bet a philosopher said that."

"Yes, Susan Coolidge. But you didn't give me a chance to say what it was she said. She might have written it just for you."

"Comfort me, then."

"It's called 'Begin Again' and it goes like this:

'Every day is a fresh beginning.
  Every morn is the world made new;
You are weary of sorrow and sinning,
  Here is a beautiful hope for you–
  A hope for me and a hope for you.' "

"Yes, well? The comfort?"

"That's it–that's the wonderful thing about your being back here: that everything that didn't quite work out the first time can be done over again. The way it should have been done *then*."

"Thanks for a glowing opportunity."

"Your eggs are ready."

"In forty seconds."

"I'll go now."

"Don't feel that you have to."

"Tomorrow is another day, Number 6."

"And tomorrow."

"And tomorrow. Toodle-oo."

In the living room the blue face winked and vanished; the speaker barked.

PART II

ESCAPE & CAPTURE

"You've been only a few days in the Village and already you think you know everything better than people who have spent their lives here . . . I don't deny that it's possible once in a while to achieve something in the teeth of every rule and tradition. I've never experienced anything of the kind myself, but I believe there are precedents for it."

The Castle, Franz Kafka

Chapter Seven

The Delivery of the Keys

He memorized the Village: each winding street, the shops, the park and sporting grounds, the gravelled access-road to the beach, and the farthest limits he might advance through the outlying meadowland before the Guardians would roll forward to establish the invisible but undeviating boundaries of his microcosmic world.

He determined, as best he could, the locations of the cameras by which his Argus-eyed jailers surveyed the wide expanse of their bucolic jail; he discovered fifty–he might have missed as many more. He also located the various concealed speakers of the public address system, an easier task since Number 2 would at odd moments during these explorations (it made no difference where he might be) address some homely piece of wisdom to him, a stale poem or a grandfatherish admonition not to walk through *that* gate, not to try the handle of *this* door. When he did walk through the gate or try the door, he would find, as often as not, that Number 2 had been having a joke with him, that there was nothing beyond or within that merited special prohibition.

In that first week he had narrowed the range of his curiosity down to the Village's two chief points of "interest" (they were the most common subjects on the picture post cards sold at the Stationer's).

The first of these was beyond question the administrative center of the Village. Once, as he had stood outside the heavy iron gates staring up at the great gray mass of the place, Number 2 had delivered over the PA system a long appreciation of this building–its functional beauty, its impregnable defenses, the Minoan complexity of its corridors, and the warmth and simplicity of his own suite of offices at the heart of the labyrinth. The encircling fence was a formidable thing, its gates patrolled by armed guards and a beige sphere acting as Cerberus at the single entrance to the building proper. ("We call him 'Rover,' " Number 2 had explained. "He's unique among the Guardians in that his design allows him to–how shall I say?–*annihilate* whoever causes him undue aggravation.")

He decided that, for the time being at least, he would not try to breach these defenses. Soon enough, Number 2 had assured him, he would be invited inside, and it was more than likely that even then his satisfied curiosity would not seem worth the price of entrance, whatever it might prove to be.

The second "point of interest" was the Village church. Twice during that first week he had entered the church in the routine course of his explorations, but though he had been somewhat taken aback to find the interior even more incongruously elegant, even more accurately Lombardic, than its facade, he had not paid it anymore attention than he would have given, just then, to an altarpiece by Cosimo Tura (an example of which, unless it were a forgery, was displayed above the main altar; it was the same, possibly, that had been stolen from the Colleoni chapel in the last days of the war.) It was lavish, it was beautiful, and though it couldn't be authentic it was entirely convincing. But it was (it had seemed) altogether unimportant.

On both occasions the church had been empty.

Then (this had been on the afternoon of that second visit) he had been sitting at his usual table at the terrace restaurant. He had been coming here at four o'clock each day to observe and to be observed. He was not ready yet to approach strangers himself (he wanted to be able, first, to distinguish between the jailers and the jailed) but he was willing they should approach him. As yet the only person who would speak to him was the blond waitress he had so unaccountably upset when he had found her crying in the kitchen. Of course, she had little choice in the matter–he was a customer who had to be served. The tweedy woman was never again at the restaurant, but her companion, the man with goitres, was often there. The goitres would leave his table just as promptly as he came to his, and on this particular afternoon, having nothing better to observe, he had watched the goitres making his way purposefully toward the steps of the church. Shortly after he had gone in at the door two other men, both as lacking in the external signs of piety as the goitres, followed him inside. After another brief interval three different men left the church.

So much bustle in and out of a building that had been empty only minutes before suggested that something else was at issue here than could be accounted for by the combined attractions of Cosimo Tura and pious exercise. After he had finished his coffee he walked to the church himself.

He found it, as he had left it, empty: the nave empty, the transepts empty, the five small side-chapels of the ambulatory empty.

There were no other doors but the one he had come in at, which he had been watching constantly since the goitres and the two other men had entered.

From that afternoon he began to make more regular visits to the church. He bought a sketchpad at the Stationer's and made studies of architectural details: the Tuscan pilasters, the caissons of the arched vault, the fine mouldings (stone, not stucco), the gigantic festooned bucranium surmounting the door–and the three cameras mounted high on the cornice 10ft below the base of the vault and 50ft above the floor, inaccessible. Together they commanded a view of the whole interior of the church, except for the darkest recesses of the first and fifth side-chapels.

Though the cameras were out of harm's way, their cables had been strung along the cornice and down the west wall (concealed by some slovenly stucco work), where they disappeared at a point just above the bucranium.

It was reassuring to find them making such simple miscalculations. This, admittedly, was only a chink in their inner defenses, but if he could discover their first error as easily as this, he would eventually find a way to breach the outer walls. He *would* escape.

In the meantime, there was this. A secondary mystery admittedly, but the unravelling of it would keep him in trim. The occasion came so soon and required so little effort that he was never able to decide, afterward, whether *they* had not in effect, handed him the keys and written out the password.

Five o'clock of a heavily overcast day: he was watching from the terrace the high breakers curl in upon themselves with a distant roar, and rush, foaming, up the shingle beach. Two figures came on to the beach at a stumbling run, carrying an orange liferaft between them. As they reached the water, a klaxon sounded. The restaurant's clientele gathered at the edge of the terrace to watch. They pointed to other figures–guards clambering down the steep descent and cheered when, just as the two fugitives had wrested the bobbing raft to the seaward side of the break-ing surf, a pastel sphere bounded into view on the access-road. Perhaps, after all, it was the fugitives they cheered–or (most likely) they were prepared to applaud pursued and pursuer indifferently, so long as either put on a good show.

The sphere hit the line of the surf at the wrong moment and was hurled back into the frothing undertow, where it spun wildly, a tire trapped in a drift of snow. The two men were in the raft now, rowing out into the heavy sea.

The klaxon continued its alarms. Guards were arriving on the beach on foot and by car. More guards were scurry-ing down the rocky paths. Other rafts were being inflated. It was a grandstand show.

He counted them as they left the church: a pair of them within moments of the klaxon's first shriek; then after an interval, the goitres.

He left his table unobtrusively and walked directly toward the church, relying on the excitement of the escape to provide his camouflage. He approached the camera that

eyed the entrance to the church, shinnied up the lamppost
on which it was mounted. With the fountain pen from his
breast pocket he squirted the camera's lens, then tamped a
bit of paper napkin on the ink-damp glass.

He mounted the steps to the church three at a time,
threw open the door, and leaped up to grasp the splayed
horns of the garlanded ox-skull. The stone held his weight
as he pulled himself up. Now, if the church were being
monitored, he could be observed, but only for—he caught
hold the cable above the bucranium, yanked—seconds.

He was, effectively, alone: the cameras defunct. For perhaps the first moment since his arrival he was unobserved.

Outside the klaxons still agonized. He wished the fugitives the best of luck—if not (for he was realistic) complete
success, then at least a quarter-hour of sustained illusion.

The high, leaded windows filtered out most of what little sunlight the day offered. Somewhere he had noticed . . .
Ah, there by the door, of course. He flicked the switch up,
and a loudspeaker coughed:

"KRAUGF! Mmmmb. You have come here," purred a
velvety voice from the vault, "seeking comfort. At these
moments when the burdens of daily life grew too heavy to
be borne alone—"

He swore. No other switch in view. He should have
thought of this before.

"—we look to a Higher Power for assistance, as children
will turn trustingly toward their loving Father. We raise our
eyes—"

To the front of the church, at a half-run. Lifted the altar
cloth, rapped the marble facing of the altar: it *sounded*
solid enough. So, the entrance to the crypt must be

concealed elsewhere; they were subtler than he would have supposed.

Then, to the side-chapels, each resplendent with its own Old Master, so that the church was a kind of digest of the major art thefts of the last quarter-century: Bellini's *Massacre of the Innocents* from the Hermitage; one of Ribera's more graphic martyrdoms (a flaying); the missing panel from the Isenheim Altarpiece, representing the temptations of St Anthony; the Rouault "Judge" from New York, and . . .

By a trick of light the fifth side-chapel was as dark as the entrance to a cavern, and by a trick of acoustics the recorded sermon here reverbed with such force that its meaning became lost in its own resonances, like the jabberwocky of a great railway terminal.

"—the perfect joy of this surrender (OR RENDER) for only by (or render) giving (FORLORNLY) up the illusion of a (UP THE HILL, forlornly) personal identity can we hope (ENTITY) to achieve real (WEEP, entity) *freedom* (EDAM! EDAM!)—"

There was something disturbing, something out of plumb about the interior of this chapel. The enfouldered darkness gave it the illusion of being much deeper than the other chapels, while in fact (yes, a glance into the Rouault chapel confirmed his suspicion) it was two to three feet shallower. The placement of the huge, time-blackened canvas on the back wall reinforced this impression (in the other chapels the paintings hung, in the usual manner, on the side walls where the light was stronger), so that the murky recessions of the painting contributed a second false depth to the chapel.

He took out his pocket torch and played its faint light across the painting. In the upper left corner, the least darkened, an oblate circle was sliced into ochrous stripes by the bars of a tall, ornamented gate, which enclosed nothing more, apparently, than this sunset. The heavy gilt lock of the gate was placed so as to provide the chief focus of interest, while off in the lower right corner, dwarfed by the rocky landscape, two figures stood, two dark silhouettes. The first, with his foot planted awkwardly upon a sharp outcropping, seemed to be trying to push away the second, who stood facing away from the viewer, a hand lifted, admonishing. In the other hand he held a small golden object.

He stepped closer to the painting; the ellipse of light tightened to a circle and intensified. Now he could recognize the painter–it was a Rubens–if not the subject. The white-bearded man seemed to be Peter. And the other figure: Christ?

Yes, for there, resting in the palm of his hand, were the two keys that he was offering to the reluctant apostle.

The painting began to move to the side with a slight squeaking sound. The light of the torch had been intense enough to have registered on the photoelectric cell behind the keys (heavily retouched by another hand) and to trigger the release mechanism.

He jumped on to the altar and stepped across the ormolu frame (copied from Boulle) on to the first iron tread of the narrow spiral staircase.

Here the light was bright as in an interrogation chamber. He poked his torch through the thick wire lattice, shattering the light bulb it guarded.

Five steps farther down, a second bulb, and twelve steps

on, the third. Pitch-darkness, and he heard above him the whirr and squeak of the painting moving back into its frame, the last muffled words of the sermon:

"—within this new hierarchy (IRE) of values (key of) lies the key to (LIES) the sturdy edifice (lies, dead) of our moralit—"

Silence, and the darkness. He continued the descent.

Chapter Eight

Twice Six

Into:

A corridor:

A sequence of doors. Above, just out of reach, parallel tracks of neon insisted on the raw whiteness of the walls. Far off, where the corridors bent, a single element, six feet of glass-tubed gas, flickered mortally.

Locked. And locked. And locked. And locked. And locked.

The sixth door opened.

A room: metal files. An iron garden-table and three iron chairs flaked white paint on to the concrete floor. On the table: a mug of coffee, still lukewarm; a Martina ashtray brimming butts; a crumpled Senior Service package; a box of safety matches; a Japanese paperback (he could not read the characters); three Danish girlie magazines; a plastic box of transistor elements; a ring of keys numbered from 2 to 15.

They keys unlocked the files; the files contained

canisters of film. Each canister was stenciled with a red numeral (from 2 to 15), followed by smaller black code-letters. There were seventeen canisters marked with a red 6. He opened, at random, 6-SCHIZ Squinting, he studied frames of the film against the light.

His face? And from this angle, the same or another?

Then: mustached, hair darkened–him? Or only a good facsimile? His judgment oscillated between credence and doubt. Yes it was he/No it was not.

Without a projector it would take days to examine all the footage contained in these seventeen canisters. And he had . . . minutes?

There was a second door. Which opened to darkness and a voice said:

"Negative."

There was a scream, piercing, a woman's. He eased the door back but did not, quite, close it; he listened at the crack:

The voice, a man's: "Shall we try that again? Necessity."

And hers, unsteady: "Inter–" A choking sound. "No, inven–"

"Please, Number 48. Just give the very first word that comes to you.

"Intervention?"

"That's better, much better. Now: pluck."

"Courage."

"Negative."

And her scream.

His voice: "Again, Number 48: pluck."

"Cour–"

"Negative."

The scream.

"Again? Pluck."

"I . . . eye . . . eyebrow."

"Very good! We're making progress today, Number 48."

Inchmeal, as this dialogue continued, he widened the crack: darkness, and still darkness, though with a faint flicker of bluish light, like the death-throes of neon. Neither speaker in the darkened room seemed to notice the intrusion.

"Now, Number 48: courage."

"I . . . no, I can't!"

"Courage."

"C–Ca–Collage."

"Continue with the sequence, Number 48."

He recognized the woman (wires twined into the shingled red-dyed hair, thick body strapped to the chair) shown on the screen as his confidante of a week earlier, the tweedy companion (the wife?) of the goitred man. Had it been the goitres who had left the film to play on unwitnessed in this room? And for what purpose, other than his idle amusement, had he been watching the documentation of this woman's torture?

"Collage," she said. "Cabbage . . . Kale . . ." The camera moved in to a close close-up, then tightened to a shot of her wounded eyes, eyes that stared, dilated, into a flickering light.

"Curtain . . . Cur-cour-age . . . Cottage . . . Cottage." The words she spoke seemed to crumble into their component syllables as they left her lips.

The man's voice: "Courage? Please respond, Number 48! Courage."

"Curdle! Curdle . . . curd . . . el . . ."

"Go on: curd."

"Cord . . . Core . . . Ca–Ck-ck-ck–"

"Core?"

The camera backed away to show the flaccid red lips, the powdered flesh eroded by sweat and tears, the jaw chewing slowly on unspoken words, and in her staring eyes a vague lust for the end of this pain, for nonexistence.

Then, abruptly, a blackness across which a dotted yellow line graphed an optimistic ascent toward the upper right corner: beneath, in bold letters:

NUMBER 48

Day 4

Pre-Terminal Aphasic Therapy.

The film ended. The tag-end of the reel flapped in the projector's beam, and the screen blinked a semaphore of black/white/black until he found the switch, flicked it OFF.

And ON, the overhead light.

Beneath the empty canister for *Day 4* were six others; the last day–7–was labeled *Termination and Review.* He replaced the film in its container in the same manner he had once, years ago (he remembered this entire era of his life intact), prepared a package of the personal effects of a friend (gored by shrapnel) to send back to his widow in Châlons-sur-Marne.

Threading the film of 6-SCHIZ into the projector, he wondered if it had been only that brief exchange on the terrace, the message scribbled on a napkin, those few guarded words, that had convinced the jailers of this place to perform their macabre "therapy." Would other Villagers be asked to pay as high a price for his friendship–for even such a small gesture in that direction?

And, if they were, could *he*, in justice–

A point of ethics he would have to consider at some later time, for now the numbers flashed backward to zero on the screen, and he saw himself waking, walking to a mirror, and staring at the image it recorded with an expression of disbelief and, to a surprising degree, terror.

A wide face that could have been called (and often had been) Slavic, though anyone who has known the Midlands would recognize the type: the fine brown hair that a single day of sunlight could dull to ash-blond; the rough modeling of brow, cheeks and nose, sturdy Saxon craftsmanship but scarcely a work of art; the thinness of the upper lip that opposed the fullness and slight thrust of the lower; the swag of flesh at the back of his jaw, a detail that had been coded into his family's genes for generations. It was a serviceable face–not especially noticeable until you noticed it, but (in his line of work) all the more serviceable for that reason. It could express, most easily, stubbornness (indeed, whatever else it might express, that stubbornness would remain, a permanent qualification), but never anything that could be called elegance. Fortunately he had never wanted to be called elegant.

Such was the face that, without paying particular attention to the matter, he was accustomed to. But *this* face, the face on the screen, was this his, too? And (cutting to another shot, in another room) *this* one?

In the first sequence all the details seemed correct. His hair was the right color; he wore it so. The clothes fit his body, the smile fit his face. But the eyes...? The eyes seemed, somehow, amiss. But of course we only know our image from a mirror, unspontaneously; perhaps our unrehearsed expressions are quite different.

The second face was less obviously his own. The hair

was darker, parted on the left. This face wore a mustache, though with apparent discomfort, for his hand (his left hand) kept reaching up to touch it, to tug at it, to test its reality. Yet apart from these merely cosmetic differences it was (it seemed to be) his face, his own.

Then: a shot of himself (mustached) walking down a street of the Village—or was it merely *a* village? Though the candy cottages on each side of the street resembled those he knew here, there were subtle differences in the warp of the land, the silhouettes of trees, the angle of the light. A seasonal difference? Or could there be, for villages as for people, such elaborate facsimiles that only by these slight tokens could the original be distinguished from its reproduction?

The man walking down the street wore a badge on his lapel that identified him as Number 12. Well, if they had to choose a number for his double, it could only be that.

Two stills, side by side: this same "Number 12" in a barber's chair. First, mustached, his darker hair parted on the left; then, shaven, the hair lightened to its natural (or was it, in this case, natural?) color, parted on the right.

Then: himself—one of these two selves—in a room of bland modernity, sprawled on a modular sofa, looking very much at home, or doing a fair job seeming so. His other self entered at the door.

"What the devil . . ." his other self said. Surely for *one* of them the surprise must have been feigned. He wished that he were not such a good actor, though of course it would be the double who would be required to act, his own reaction the "genuine" one. No?

They approached each other until the camera included both in a medium close-up. They wore on the lapels of their identical jacket badges with the numeral 6. He could not be certain, seeing them together, which of them had been shown as 12 in the earier footage. Had he seen an episode like this in anymore conventional theater, were he not already convinced that *he* had been one of the principles, he would immediately have assumed that this was nothing but trick photography, an actor playing a double role.

The self who had just entered nodded, smiling a thin smile (his). "Oh, very good. Very, very good. One of Number 2's little ideas, I suppose. Where'd he get you–from Xerox? Or are you one of these double agents we hear so much about?"

His smile, and the voice his too.

The other replied (smiling the same smile, speaking in the same voice): "Since you've gone to so much trouble, the least I can do is offer you a drink."

"Scotch."

And (he thought) on the rocks, by preference.

The one who'd made the offer went to the wrong cabinet; his doppelganger, almost apologetically, corrected the mistake.

As they faced the bar, their faces turned from the camera, one of them said: "I take it I'm supposed to go all fuzzy around the edges and rush into the distance screaming 'Who am I?' "

Was *that* the way he talked? He hoped not but he wasn't sure.

"Ice?"

"Please. Oh, careful! Not from the kitchen, you know. That's an ice-bucket on the second shelf."

They toasted. Again their two opposing profiles filled the screen. Each man studied his mirror image.

"Do you know–I never realized I had a freckle on the side of my nose. Tell you what, when they film my life story, you get the part." He turned. The camera followed him. "Cigar? Ah-ah! With the right hand, yes? Yes. And that wasn't what *I* would have chosen for myself. Most people find my taste too individual, so I carry those as a courtesy. Also, they made a slight mistake with your hair–it's a shade too light."

The other: "It's not going to work, you know. I have a particularly strong sense of identity."

Yes, he thought, he did/I do. Provisionally he accorded this one (the sprawler on the couch, the fumbler at the liquor cabinet) the distinction of being his True Self; the other must be, then, the Double.

The Double answered: "*You* have?" And laughed: in pitch, in timber, in rhythm it was his laugh. "Oh yes, I forgot for a moment–you're supposed to be me. You're Number 6, the goodie, and I'm the baddie who's trying to break you down. Right?"

It might also be maintained against this Double that his dialogue was bad, but then his own reply was not much better:

"Right. Only there's no *suppose* about it."

"Another drink?"

And so they continued, in close-up and medium close-up, their war of wit, until one of them (he'd lost track, by then, which was which) proposed a more effective test: they would duel.

It developed into a minor pentathlon. In all the events the one he'd elected to be the True Self came in a poor second. His score on the electronic pistol range was six hits to the

Double's perfect ten. When they fenced (not without appropriate references to *Hamlet*, Act 5, scene 2), the True Self's movements were overwrought, rough, even desperate, while the Double executed each thrust and parry with consummate ease, as (he pointed this out himself) one would expect of a fencer on the Olympics team.

"If ever I challenge you to a duel in earnest," he said, the tip of his foil pressed against the other's throat, "your best chance would be battle axes in a dark cellar."

They raced, but of this the cameras had recorded only the finish: the Double's triumph, his own chagrin, the resulting fight—and his further chagrin. He was spared from a definitive defeat only by the arrival of one of the Guardians, which shepherded them toward the Village's administration center.

Cut to:

The office of Number 2. Here the modernity was anything but bland; it was the nightmarish progeny of the union of the Ziegfield Follies and IBM. It assaulted the senses, attacked taste, made pageants of plastic and Day-Glo paint. Was this the "warmth and simplicity" that Number 2 had boasted of?

Was this, for that matter, Number 2? This stripling youth, in hornrim glasses, dithering on in that pure Oxonian accent that only a few Fulbright scholars ever master? So—since the events of this film there had been at least one shuffling of the staff. It was another evidence of their weakness, and he welcomed it.

Cut to:

Himself, or his double, strapped and wired into the chair (or its double) in which Number 48 had received her "aphasic therapy." Dilated irises reflected the blinking light.

The voice of (the anterior) Number 2: "Who are you?"

And he: "Would you mind switching that idiot light out? I'm getting cramps."

"Who" (very owllike, his who) "are you?"

"You know who I am. I'm Number 6."

"Where do you come from?"

"You know that too."

"How did you get here?"

"Ah! Now there's something you'd know better than I. I was unconscious at the time, if you remember."

The irises flared with a brighter burst of light, and his lip curled back in pain.

"What was your purpose in coming here?"

More and more, he decided as he watched *this* Number 2 go on, he preferred his own. If nothing else, he was a better entertainer.

"I had none. I'll go away if you like."

This time, at the cue of light, he cried aloud.

"How did your people know that Number 6 was here?"

"What people?"

"How did they know enough about *him* to produce *you*?"

"I don't understand."

Number 2, mildly: "What were you doing in the recreation room?"

"Showing this synthetic twin of mine how to shoot and fence."

So: this was the one he had supposed was ersatz. Then why (again the light flared, and he writhed in an agony that could not have been faked) were they torturing *this* one?

"For the last time, what do you people want with Number 6?"

And, screaming: "*I'm* Number 6, you sadist! *I'm* Number

6, you know I'm Number 6. I'm Number 6, I'm Number 6, I'm Number 6, I'm Number 6." Until, mercifully, he fainted.

He checked his watch. It was now fifteen minutes since he'd seen the three guards leaving the church, the limit he had set to this investigation, and half the reel still remained. Would he be cautious, then, or curious?

There was this to be said for caution-that he could never, in any case, stay to see all seventeen instalments of the serial; even if he could, it might be that he would learn only so much from it as his jailers wished him to know. The film seemed carefully edited-but to what purpose, on whose behalf? There had been something (he had known this all along) too pat about this undertaking, as though it had all been prearranged-the false escape, the alarm, his discovery of the secret staircase, the open door to the film archives, the keys laid out on the table, the projector left running. But if they had *meant* him to see this, were they likely to interrupt him now?

Curiosity, on the other hand, did not need apologies. It had become by now his dominant passion. He resisted it only to the extent that he adjusted the Fr/Sc dial to MAX. A blur of images skittered across the screen: his face, his other face, their dialogue a jabber of chipmunks; a woman (to him unknown); the three of them careening about Number 2's office, bobbing up and down in chairs, gesturing, chirruping.

Then, a procession of geometric images almost too rapid to be seen singly-squares, circles, crosses, star, and three wavy lines. Rhine cards-the abbreviated Scripture of the ESP fanatics, though how *these* had come into it . . .

Abruptly (half an inch was left on the reel) the tone of

the film altered. He reduced the speed, backtracked, and saw:

His two selves, standing silhouetted in a cottage doorway. About them the dead black of a moonless night. The camera-work, unlike that which had preceded it, was shaky, botched, as though this one scene had not been stage-managed for the benefit of a television crew.

One of the two figures broke from the doorway (had they been fighting?) and ran across the lawn for several yards.

And stopped.

Directly before him stood one of the spheres. The street-lamp made of it a crescent of beige ("Rover" therefore) above the great, shadowed, pulsing mass. It advanced on the man who had run from the cottage; who, with terror, addressed it:

"The Schizoid Man!"

Rover rolled to a halt.

The other man stepped from the doorway and addressed the same watchword, though with more assurance, to the sphere.

It swayed and quivered, rolling toward the man in front of the cottage, then back to the other, like a wolf that stands at an equal distance above two equally attractive sheepfolds, unable to choose. The first man chose for him—he broke. He ran.

The sphere, pursuing, hit a stone in its path, sailed a few feet into the air, settled with a quiver, and swerved down the same sidestreet where the man had disappeared. The camera held the shot of the deserted street: there was a scream.

The reel ended with a final still: a tabletop, and on it a

belt-buckle, a keyring with two keys, some nails, a cigarette lighter, a few odd-shaped tiny lumps of silvery metal, and a small silver disc of the type that surgeons use in repairing fractured skulls. Presumably, but for these few artifacts, the other remnants had proved digestible.

Was it of any significance that he had never had a silver plate in his skull? (More precisely, that he did not *remember* anything of that sort?) Finally, could he never *prove* he was who he believed himself to be? Finally, can anyone? Conviction is not a proof, for he was inclined to believe that it had been the Double they had tortured, not himself, and he (the Double) had certainly been persuaded that he was Number 6. It was just that, the strength of that conviction, that made him think the man was synthetic: for he did not think that he (himself) at root would *insist* on being a mere number.

But it made no difference, really, who he was, who he had been, what he remembered and what he had been made to forget: he was himself, and he knew the interior dimensions of that self. This was sufficient.

Once again he reversed the reel. Again he watched the sphere start off after its victim, hit the rock, bound up, and settle, quivering.

There–in those three seconds of film, and not in any vortex of speculation and ravelled deceit–lay the *significance* of the thing; even if they had set up this private screening for some involuted reason of their own, they had betrayed their hand.

It was enough to make him laugh.

It remained for him to cover his tracks. He returned to the outer room and replaced all but three of the canisters

(6-SCHIZ, 6-MHR, 6-FIN) in their drawer. He removed other canisters from other drawers at random, opened them, and piled their reels of film in the middle of the floor. Threw the empty canisters into a corner, except for two (marked 2-POLIT and 14-LESB); in these he placed the reels from 6-MHR and 6-FIN. The film of 6-SCHIZ was placed at the top of the pyre.

Using the safety matches on the table, he set it alight. With luck and good ventilation the blaze might reach the file drawers he had left gaping open; it might even work through the walls and into other rooms or through the ceiling to the church. With this in mind, he propped open the door to the corridor.

He remembered another time–when? long ago, years and years–like this: a room of gutted files and the first flickering as the heaped documents began to catch; himself standing, as now, on the threshold to–where had that happened? Ostrava? Or that other town across the border, a suburb of Krakow: Skawina? Wadowice? Well, that was the past–eventually, even without assistance, one forgot the names, the dates, the faces. There were just a few bright images here and there, like the sweepings from an editing room floor.

He paused at the foot of the spiral staircase. A voice said: "What the hell?" And a second voice, the goitres: "Someone has smashed the damned *bulbs*!"

The squeak of the Rubens closing, and the slow clanking descent of the two men in darkness.

Carefully, distributing his weight among all four limbs, he twined his way up the spiral of the stairs, pressing close against the central support-pole. At the twelfth step he stopped: the footsteps were now very near, the voices only slightly farther away:

"Hey, do you smell—"

"Smoke!"

The footsteps quickened to a staccato. He reached up blindly, caught a trouser cuff, and pulled. There was almost no resistance. A scream, a thud. An obscenity silenced by a second thud, and the irregular cascade of limbs and torso down to the foot of the staircase. No, not to the foot: three more muffled bumps. There, he had reached the bottom.

"Eighty-Three?" the goitres called down into the well of darkness. "Are you . . . did you trip?"

The air was tinged with smoke that tickled his nose and throat. His heartbeat not much louder or faster than usual.

"Maybe I should . . . go . . . and warn . . ." The tone conveyed, like a Reuters photograph coded into binary blacks and whites, the image of his leg lifted at the knee, hesitating whether to place the foot on the tread above or the tread below, poised between two fears.

The foot came down on the lower tread. The goitres was more afraid, at last, of the consequences of neglected duty. He moved down into the thickening smoke by fits and starts, still calling on Number 83, who, in reply, had begun to groan.

Either his eyes were now adjusting to the darkness or some faint glimmer from the fire was lighting the stairwell, for when the foot, shod in white buckskin, came into view he could just discern it.

The goitres had not developed momentum equal to his companion's: when his leg was pulled out from under him, he fell solidly on his behind. He caught hold of the central pole, resisting the hand that would pull him farther down. He began to scream.

The buckskin shoe came off in his hands. Throwing it

aside, he clambered up the steps to the goitres' level. A hand clawed at his trousers.

The goitres' face was a gray oval above a lighter gray triangle of shirt-front. He struck him across the side of his head in a manner intended more to startle than to cause real pain. He felt no malice toward their pawns. God knew what kind of men they might have been once!

The body tumbled slowly, moaning, from tread to tread.

He raced to the top of the staircase, where the smoke with no egress, was thickest. He tried to push the painting to one side, but it stuck firmly in place. Regretfully, he kicked his way through the lower left-hand corner (the viewer's left as he faces it).

Squirmed out through this hole, hopped down from the altar to the diapered floor. He turned back to make certain he had not damaged any of the finer passages. No, the rip did not extend beyond the dark jumble of rocks. A competent restorer would have no great problem with that. From the newly-made fissure in these rocks smoke curled forth in black, baroque designs. He thought of the harrowing of hell and left the church, still unobserved, whistling a tune he hadn't remembered for years, another shard dislodged from the proper strata of memory, while inside the velveteen voice continued to promise some kind of salvation to anyone ("you") who would surrender his insignificant identity to a Higher Power, which remained unspecified.

Chapter Nine

In the Cage

According to the general report of the Villagers, the fugitives had succeeded in their escape–but by the expedient of suicide. When the sphere capsized their raft, they had been far enough from the shore so that their weighted bodies sank to a good depth; there was ample time to drown before the divers could recover them. Number 2 maintained that this was an entirely legendary acount, that in fact the fugitives had been caught warm and struggling and were presently undergoing rehabilitation.

"That's too bad," he had said.

"You would have preferred for them to be dead?" Number 2 asked.

"No, I'm not a romantic, and I don't expect death to solve any problems. It's too bad that they didn't escape."

"I'm surprised that, being there for the beginning, you didn't stay to see the finish. Where did you go, by the way?"

"An escape is as private a matter as lovemaking. As I'm

not a voyeur, I went home. You mean to say there are actually minutes of the day your cameras aren't watching me?"

"Oh, I have the report somewhere, but asking you is easier. It's tedious study, cataloguing your habits, Number 6. You rise at seven, put on water for tea, shower, dress, drink your tea. Then, at seven-fifteen, you run to the beach for a quarter-hour of calisthenics. Then–should I go on?"

"I'll admit it isn't an inspiring theme. Now, if I were living somewhere else, I might put on a better show, with more variety."

"Which reminds me–when are *you* going to attempt *your* escape?"

"Soon, Number 2, soon."

"This inaction isn't like you."

"On the other hand, I'm not impetuous. When I do make my break, I expect to get through to the other side."

"To freedom, eh?"

"To freedom."

Number 2 chuckled. "Ah, it's little moments like this that make it all seem worth the effort. Don't abandon your ideals too easily, Number 6. Hold them up proudly, and show your pluck."

He paused to study his listener's response to this key word from Number 48's therapy. "Doesn't that word . . . ring any bells for you?"

"Should it? Was it the theme of one of your recitations?"

Number 2 sighed. A stalemate. "No, not that I recall, Number 6, but I'll see if I can't dig something up."

He made the promised escape two weeks later, a month from the day of his arrival. It had been carefully planned, the detail-work accomplished during the hours of curfew and the necessary apparatus cached at the eastern perimeter of the beach. The sheer rockface that bounded the beach all along its length pressed forward here into the sea. One could continue beyond this point only by taking to the water (and he knew that the bay was well-patrolled, that any escape by this route was almost guaranteed to fail) or by scaling the rocks, an action certain to call oneself to the attention of the Guardian that shepherded that sector of the plateau above.

The advantage of this position was its isolation. Villagers seldom ventured here, for the water was rough, the shingle more than usually coarse, and the prospect seaward without any picturesque merit. It was also, because of the cul de sac formed by the cliff, the outermost point from the Village to which one could advance without being turned back by the Guardians.

He stood, that morning, at the base of the cliff, surveying for the last time the line of ascent he had marked out.

7:20 am.

The sea heaved and shattered against the cliff. The cliff's shadow slid eastward by imperceptible degrees across the wet shingle. A muck of oil that had been steadily encroaching on the beach these past two weeks (a freighter must have foundered nearby during the storm) writhed amorphously at the water's edge, prismed, bubbled.

He climbed quickly to the first ledge, unravelling as he advanced nylon cord from a thick spool. The other end of the cord was knotted about his bundle of equipment.

The second stage was the most dangerous, though it did not take him to any very dizzying height, for here he had to move out along rocks drenched by the breaking surf. Twice his shoes slipped on the wet sandstone, and twice as he sought for a handhold the projecting rock tore loose, like a child's rotted milk-tooth, to vanish into the white turbulence below.

At the next ledge, forty feet above the beach, he paused for breath and dried the soles of his shoes with a handkerchief.

A gull leaped from a cranny in the rocks below and rode the updraft on a long arc, wings taut. As it sliced the air inches from his face, it screamed. A flicker of sentient black beads. And gone.

He had never seen another gull along the beach, nor in the town any birds but sparrows and pigeons. Had he been a believer in omens, he would have supposed this a good one.

7:24.

Without a pause at the third ledge, he scrambled up the last ten feet to stand, panting, on the ratchel, in sunlight. Grass stretched on before him to the south and west, a pastoral vacancy that reverberated with the crash of the waves on the sea-wall.

Where the cliff's overhang allowed him to draw up his equipment without danger of snagging it in the rocks, he drew the cord tight, tighter. It accepted the strain (as it had in his earlier tests) and the bundle rose, with a slow pendulous swing, from the beach far below.

Then (7:31): it lay spread out before him in the grass–a sack of food, twenty-odd lengths of curved aluminum tubing, and an adjustable spanner. Still no sign of a Guardian. He needed five minutes to assemble the cage, five minutes, and then let them bowl their whole armada at him. If, that is, there was any truth in Euclid's geometry.

He grabbed the spanner and set to work.

The sphere (it was baby-blue with a few lavender spots of acne) stopped short some thirty feet ahead. Always before at its appearance he had headed back like an obedient sheep to the Village.

"Budge me," he said. "Just try."

The oblate hemisphere of the cage was planted in the earth four feet behind him; not much farther behind the cage-the cliff's edge.

He would allow the thing five minutes to make a charge. Then, if it proved too patient or too wise, he would set off without that particular satisfaction.

To taunt the sphere (did they have some kind of robotic—and woundable—ego programmed into them?) he cast small rocks at it, which bounced harmlessly off its hide. (Plastic? Probably.) The sphere quivered, just as (he hoped) a bull, its rage building, would paw at the dust.

He dashed to the right, to the left, without, however, straying more than a few feet from his cage at any time. (El Cordobes, clowning close beside the barreras.) The sphere echoed his movements uncertainly, approached to twenty feet, to fifteen feet. He flung the largest of the rocks. Where it struck another lavender blotch slowly spread across the baby-blue. Then, if it had been a bull, it would have bellowed; it charged. He threw himself behind the cage.

Too late, as though it realized its error, it tried to slow. Too late: it struck the cage broadside, deforming at the impact. (The cage held.) The sphere's momentum carried it up across the arched tubing and, cresting the small dome, still up, and out.

He turned on to his back to watch it sail forth, blue against blue, into the vacant air, and drop (had it been alive, it would have screamed) toward the roaring confrontation of sea and cliff, of sea and cliff, and, now, sphere.

There was an explosion. One could just trace its outlines amid the continuing tumult. So, the things were mortal. He hadn't expected that.

The assembled cage stood a bit over three feet high, with a diameter at its base of seven feet. The 35 pounds of tubing, pilfered from the terrace restaurant (they had supported the umbrellas over the tables, the awning above the bandstand), described lines of longitude and latitude with diagonal struts to reinforce major points of stress. Though not as sturdy as a geodesic dome, this design required fewer joints and was therefore easier to assemble. Even so, its construction had occupied four hours of each night for the last two weeks.

For easier carrying it could be disassembled into three pieces, but he could also carry it, as he did now, tortoise-fashion, on his shoulders. He walked at a steady pace, for the slightest break in his stride tended to make the carapace tilt and snag a foot in the grass. His arms ached from the cruciform attitude required to keep it balanced, but caution was to be preferred to comfort. The next sphere might appear in an hour or in the next minute: until he was certain he had reached safe ground (and he didn't know yet whether he could, whether the Village was established on the mainland), he could not afford to let down his defenses.

It was noon before the second sphere evidenced itself. This one was beige.

"Hello there, Rover," he called out, quickening his pace. The sphere followed at a considerate distance, sometimes shooting out on a tangent from its direct course in a sudden burst of speed, at other times describing broad loops or bouncing. Its erratic, whimsical zigzagging reminded him of a puppy at play.

At one o'clock he chose a level of ground and pulled the cage down about him firmly. Then he opened his makeshift knapsack and took out the lunch he'd prepared–a roast beef sandwich, pickles, two deviled eggs, and a pop-top can of soda.

Rover rolled up to the edge of the cage. Tentatively, sphere pushed at hemisphere. Joints creaked. It pressed harder, and beige skin bulged in through the squares and triangles of the lattice. He sipped his soda and watched the sphere slowly mount the mound above him and roll to the other side.

Then, a second time, with a running start that carried it over the top and several feet into the air. It landed with the sound of a fat body unstuck from a bathtub.

The third time it tried to climb the lattice of the cage as slowly as possible. Halfway up, miscalculating the force required, it collapsed back to the ground.

The cage had withstood each test without any sign of weakening.

The sphere withdrew to a normal conversational distance, and a voice said:

"Well, Number 6, I have to give you credit. This is a splendid idea, splendidly executed."

He looked around, but there was no one, nothing visible but himself and the sphere amid all this green uniformity, yet it *had* been the voice of Number 2, and, as the sphere shook like a bowl full of beige jelly, his laugh.

"Haunted?" Number 2 asked.

"Oh, another advance in technology. Where do you put the speaker, if you don't mind my asking?"

"This whole thing is just a membrane, you know, and then, what with the miracle of transistors . . . I can take the volume up to something unbelievable–LIKE THIS:

THE THING THAT GOES THE FARTHEST

TOWARDS MAKING LIFE WORTHWHILE,

THAT COSTS THE LEAST AND DOES THE MOST,

IS JUST A PLEASANT SMILE . . .

"But," he went on, sniffing, much subdued, "I have to remember to adjust the audio pickup on this end when I do that. It's much worse for me, with these earphones, than for you out there in the pasture with your picnic basket. I always seem to be interrupting your meals."

"It's your most excusable fault, Number 2."

"May I ask you a personal question, Number 6?"

"By all means! Let's have no secrets between *us*!"

"It's about Number 127, the young lady with whom you had arranged a tryst this morning. I was wondering what *lure* you used to persuade her to come to such a strange place, at such an odd hour."

"Ah, how is she?"

"*This* is a fine time to show your concern! After sending her out to the meadow–and heaven knows what you'd led her to expect–as your *decoy*. She's back, a little sadder and wiser, but none the worse for wear. In fact, I think . . . let me see which camera is . . . yes, she's already back at her job. The restaurant should take her mind off your betrayal for a little while, but I'm certain she will never trust you again."

"She probably will never see me again. But if you would like to apologize to her on my behalf, I would appreciate it."

"I already explained to her that you were only following our instructions. That seemed to cheer her up a little."

"If I could have come up with any other way to divert Boy-Blue's attention, I would never have–"

"Yes, yes, I know: ends and means. People are only pawns in your ruthless bid for power, eh, Number 6?"

"For freedom, rather. And far from being ruthless, I think I've shown great restraint."

"You call arson restraint?"

"Arson? Did I leave something heating on the stove?"

"And the wanton destruction of equipment worth . . . well, I won't say how much."

"Boy-Blue, you mean? It didn't show that much restraint about destroying my equipment, which is irreplaceable, after all. It was quite ready to herd *me* over the cliff."

"That was an error, however. It was on auto-pilot, and though its sensory apparatus et cetera would have sufficed in most circumstances, it was simply unaware of the drop-off. The Guardians can sense objects and discriminate shapes, even in the infrared spectrum, but the *absence* of an object requires some larger degree of sophistication. It shouldn't have charged, of course, and had I been forced to choose between you and it, I'd agree that you're less easy to replace and therefore more valuable."

"You flatter me."

"But that doesn't excuse your taunting the poor thing."

"Well, perhaps I am ruthless. I'll tell you what–when we come to the *next* cliff–"

The beige sphere emitted a dry chuckle. "Oh, we can't allow you to repeat your successes. Rover isn't on auto-pilot: I'm in charge now. And our engineers are already making modifications to insure against any future repetition of such an error. But why am I telling *you* all this? Really, I'm too candid with you, Number 6. You draw me out. What is the secret of your charm? It's unnatural of me, your jailer, to deal with you on terms approaching equality. Don't you agree?"

"That it's unnatural? Quite. But unnaturalness–I thought that was the whole point of the Village."

"You're being semantic again, Number 6. What I meant was quite simple, heart-warming even. I feel an *affinity* for you–I have from the first. And admit it, Number 6, don't you feel something of the same sort for me?"

He glanced up quizzically at the huge sphere, which rolled forward a few inches across the grass, as a dog will step nearer when it is expecting to be scratched. "Well, I can say this much–nothing human is alien to me."

The sphere breathed a sigh, a brief hiss of gas before the puncture sealed itself. "That rather begs the question, but I won't press the matter. As for me, I have always found *everything* human to be alien. But this is all philosophy, and though I enjoy a little philosophy just before I go to bed, it sorts ill with heroic endeavor. Have you finished your lunch? Are you ready to continue this doomed escape? I am. This is quite a holiday for me, you know. I've never run one of these contraptions before. The sensation can't be described."

Indescribably, the sphere bounced up and down in place.

"All right. Why don't you back up some twenty yards or so, and I will be able to walk on much more comfortably. If you come too near, I shall have to go along at a crouch."

"But our conversation."

"Just raise your volume."

The sphere backed away with evident reluctance. "Here?"

"A little farther, I think."

"HERE?"

"There, and now—" He glanced at his watch (1:36 pm), strapped on the pack, and lifted the aluminum cage from the ground. Balancing the cage on his shoulders, he set off to the southeast. "—freedom or bust."

The sphere followed at the agreed distance. Number 2 had switched the audio to the regular Muzak tape that was constantly broadcasted over the Village PA system. Unconsciously, the sphere bobbed and his feet marched to the varying tempos of Sigmund Romberg's *Desert Song*.

3:20.

Two horizons: the first, an ochrous line of scrub, marked the limit of the foreground, so near that he could distinguish even from here the few late blossoms on the branches of the gorse and the guelder rose; the second, above this, was a thin wavering stripe of ultramarine—a pine forest. How far ahead, or what might still lie before it, he did not stop to consider.

He did not stop. He walked, crouched, never raising the cage more than a foot off this rougher ground, pocked with holes, dotted with boulders, intent on just the few yards directly ahead of him, careful of his own and his cage's footing.

The sphere, taking advantage of the irregular terrain, followed him closely or moved ahead in order to deflect him toward the rockier patches of ground, ready to rush against the cage whenever the lay of the land might make it the least bit vulnerable. It need not overturn the cage to succeed; it was enough, by attrition, to disable it, to bear down on it when some dip in the earth or spine of rock prevented an equal distribution of the load. Cripples are easy prey.

And so he did not notice when the simple green horizon behind him generated the first telltale dot, the merest whirring gnat; did not notice even the gnat grown, at ten o'clock before its zenith, to a hawk's stature. Only when the shadow of its segmented body lay, flickering, in the dry grass ahead did he pay it any heed.

The helicopter hovered, describing a slow conical helix that narrowed and lowered toward him with gentle persuasiveness.

To the right the warp and wrinkle of the ground that arched up to the ocher horizon was less pronounced. The sphere, as he angled toward this smoother passage, darted ahead and planted its bulk before him. He veered left. The sphere rolled closer, pressed itself against the bars of the cage with force enough to bring them both to a stop but not so much that it would be propelled up and across the dome of the cage. It had learned the precise balance of thrust and counterthrust required to achieve equilibrium.

Little by little, he sidled the cage about the sphere, a small gear circling about a larger. Eventually the sphere had to concede another few yards of ground, but, so long as it persisted, never much more. Again it would station itself in his path, again he would be forced to revolve the cage's cogs about the base of the sphere. The sphere could not finally prevent his progress, but it could, and did, reduce the speed of his advance to a glacial crawl.

The helicopter depended directly overhead, deafening. Its rotors sliced at the molecules of the air, a sword-dance above the tiny, struggling Damocles below.

Again the sphere approached, and just as it would have pressed itself against the cage, he shifted the bars sideways. The sphere skimmed over one side, plopped into a boulder, bounced, and rolled several feet down the slope before it recovered its wits. He had gained a dozen yards meanwhile. He reversed his course, and the sphere bounded over the crown of the cage, landed with a damp smack, bounced high, and bobbed even farther down the slope. A gain, this time, of almost twenty yards.

Growing cautious, the sphere circled some distance ahead and bore down on him slowly until again sphere and cage were locked in their abstract embrace and again he had to begin the laborsome business of revolving the cage inch by inch across the resisting grass, the gouged earth: though he made certain at regular intervals that the joints were tight, he knew the aluminum latticework could not hold out against this kind of strain.

At 4:30 pm he was still fifty feet from the crest of the slope. It had taken an hour and ten minutes to cover 300 yards of ground (half that distance discounting the diversions and false starts that the terrain and the sphere had forced on him).

But now Rover seemed to undergo a sudden change of heart. It sailed up the hill on a smooth arc, its great beige bulk all atremble from the unequalness of the land. It topped the ridge, dropped from sight, then rose on a high skyward bounce, a swift beige idea of a flower, fell behind the ridge, rose again, though to a lesser height, and called out in a tenor voice that rivaled the bass of the helicopter:

"BRAVO!"

And, on the third bounce, lower, louder:

"MOLTO BRAVO!"

And finally, with just one hemisphere rising over the hilltop:

"WELL DONE, NUMBER 6! WELL DONE!"

At the top of the hill he thought of Moses on the bank of Jordan. He stood at a brink no tortoise could ever negotiate, a drop of twenty feet to the rocky ground, not sheer but steep enough to make the cage worse than useless.

The sphere bounced itself out, diminuendo of a Japanese drum.

"No, no, no!" it grumbled at a sane decibel level. "Not *now*, Number 19! Fly away home, and I'll whistle when I need you. Can't you see he's still full of *hope*?"

The helicopter canted left and rose to vanish at the horizon that had engendered it.

"And now, Number 6–how do you intend to get down *here* without being tipped out of that shell of yours? Eh? Eh?"

"I'm thinking."

"The fault extends to your left for a good mile and for longer than that on your right. Of course, you *could* try and take your chances here."

"No, I'll take your word instead." He set off toward the left.

"You mean it–you really *are* taking my word! Oh, you

sly fox! Do you know what I'm going to do just for that? What nice reward? I'll move off *way* down over there (oh, I keep forgetting I can't point–there, toward those hills) and let you lower your shell by its cord and climb down after it. In perfect safety, undisturbed. Isn't that big of me?"

"Number 2, you're a peach."

The sphere laughed uncertainly.

"I'm waiting for my reward."

It bounded off, beige on tawny green, toward the pine slopes, a mile across the intervening plain.

He lowered the cage by the nylon cord, eyeing the sphere carefully meanwhile to see whether it would swoop to the bait.

From the distance a tiny voice called to him: "YOU HAVE MY WORD."

The cage settled upside-down. He threw the cord after it and scrambled down the incline at breakneck speed. At the bottom he quickly set the cage upright, safely enturtled once again.

The sphere had not stirred. Its tiny voice called out: "READY?"

He started off in the direction of the pines. Two miles? Three?

"READY OR NOT!" The sphere rolled toward him, but preserved a comfortable distance, although the ground here was as uneven as it had been on the other side of the fault.

"Not so much as a thank-you?" Number 2 asked.

"Does the mouse thank the cat?"

"Perhaps a very clever mouse would."

"Clever mice–do they taste better?"

The sphere reproduced, highly amplified, a sound of smacking lips.

* * *

5:30 pm.

The hills were tantalizingly near. He cursed the long midsummer day, which he had been thankful for till now. Until darkness offered him an equivalent defense, he hadn't wanted to abandon the cage.

Number 2, who had been mumbling something to himself for the last mile about the Lake Poets (he seemed to have it in mind to bring them to the Village for rehabilitation), suddenly stepped up his volume and gargled for his attention.

"I hope you're beginning to get some idea, at last, of the futility of this adventure of yours."

"I thought it was the other kind of attitude you wanted to encourage in me, Number 2—my idealism, my resolution, my optimism."

"Oh, those things are fine to talk about, and the entertainment industry would be ruined without them. But there are times one must be serious and despair. Not of everything, of course, but of these treacherous, abstract ideas. Freedom! As though we weren't all determinists these days! Where, in this vastly overpopulated world, is there even *room* to be free? No, Number 6, though you may clang your bells for freedom, the best that you can escape to is some more camouflaged form of imprisonment than we provide, though we do try to be unobtrusive. Freedom? Perhaps there was a time long ago, a Golden Age, when men were free, but I see as little sign of that utopia in the past as in the future."

"So much philosophy, Number 2. It must be close to your bedtime."

"Philosophy? Psychology rather, or literature. My

arguments aren't based on reason but on the particular situation you find yourself in at this moment, sustaining, with ever-increasing difficulty, the illusion that you are escaping."

"If I can sustain the illusion long enough, it would be as good as a reality. That's Bishop Berkeley. I should think that jailers must experience a larger degree of futility than even the most degraded prisoner. A prisoner can take refuge in the consciousness of the injustice done him, and for him there are at least *fantasies* of freedom. But the jailer is sentenced to his jail for life: he and his jail form an identity. Every one of his prisoners might escape, but *he* would still be left, a jailer in a jail, the prisoner of a tautology. The very best he can hope for is to make his jail perfect—that is to say, escape-proof—but the manacles he loads with iron are locked to his own wrists. No, if it's a question of futility, I'd rather be a prisoner any day."

"All that you say, Number 6, is half true. Mine is not an enviable lot. It is, indeed, futile at times, but a little futility never hurt anyone. It's homeopathic medicine for the larger futility of Life with a capital L. However, there are *some* advantages in my situation. There is pleasure in the exercise of power, and more pleasure in the exercise of more power. I can hope not only to perfect my prison—our prison, I should say—but also to fill it with more and more and more prisoners, until finally—but it would not be modest to say that."

"Until finally you have made the whole world a single prison."

"It almost makes me sound like an idealist, doesn't it? My intention was only to demonstrate that even jailers have their dreams, and a jailer's dreams are, in a practical sense, more realizable than a prisoner's. The moral of that, Number 6, you may draw yourself."

"An offer of employment?"

"Possibly. Your qualifications are evident: you have initiative, intelligence, experience of the world. You lack only acceptable character references, but that could be worked on. If your interest is sincere, what better moment to demonstrate it than now, you are still, putatively, escaping?"

"Speaking of my escape—look: we've almost reached the woods."

"Yes, I was about to mention that myself. It means that I shall have to *press* you for a reply. You are still free to return, free to join us."

"Thanks, but if it's all the same, I'd rather be free to be free."

"You intend to return, then, to London?"

"Not then—now."

"And there, what will you do?"

"Contact the authorities."

"You see, immediately you leave *our* jail, you fly to *theirs*! I'm sorry, Number 6, but I really cannot allow that."

The beige sphere made a sudden rush.

Squatting, he pulled the cage down about him. The sphere swerved and interposed itself between the cage and the woods, pressed itself against the bars.

"We've been all through this, Number 2. The woods aren't fifty yards away. You've lost."

The beige sphere began to pulse at a rapid tempo. Its south pole depressed and darkened to chocolate-brown.

"You won't reconsider, Number 6?"

"Not even if you threaten to turn to Golden Syrup and candy me. Sorry, pal."

"Well then, adieu," said the sphere, and shot high, *high* into the air.

"Finally," he muttered. He slipped the three false joints from the carefully sharpened poles and swung them on their hinges. Then, as the sphere reached the apogee of its ascent, he slipped out from the cage and begun running to the woods. He had not gone twenty yards when the sphere smashed into the cage with a loud metallic groan (the cage collapsing) and a plastic burp (the sphere punctured).

He turned to see the sphere gradually metamorphose into an ellipsoid, as it writhed, impaled, on the three spikes. It flopped softly to its side, and shook the wreckage of the cage from its wrinkling hide. Half its surface now was lavender, with scarlet pox-marks where the pikes had entered.

The hissing changed to a bubbling whistle, a flute clogged with spittle. Rather, a trio of flutes, which one by one abandoned their shrill, monotonous song. The damned things were self-sealing!

He started running, for his life.

The sphere bellowed at him: "FUM BLOOH EH SCHPUSH UFH! SHUH BEPPEP!" and lumbered liquidly after. Even half-deflated, it could slop along at a fair clip, but he reached the woods with yards to spare and stood once more encaged by the gigantic bars of the pines.

The sphere somehow was managing to re-inflate itself. It addressed him earnestly: "WABE, NUBBER SHES! WABE A MINNUB!"

He wabed, and in a minubb the sphere had reassumed its earlier, Euclidean proportions, though all but a little patch at the top was lavender now.

"Thank you," Number 2 said. "I wanted, before you went off, to extend my congratulations and—"

"If that's all, then I really must—"

"*And* to say that I've found that poem you asked me to dig up. So if you will wait just a moment..."

"Why not send a copy to my address in London?"

"Because it's very apposite to the present occasion. If I may?"

"Is it long?"

"Just six lines. It's called 'Pluck Wins.' Listen:

'Pluck wins! It always wins! though days be slow
And nights be dark 'twixt days that come and go.
Still pluck will win; its average is sure,
He gains the prize who will the most endure,
Who faces issues; he who never shirks,
Who waits and watches, and who always works.' "

At the northern horizon he saw the gnat that would become the hawk that would become the helicopter.

"That was nice, Number 2, but now I really must say goodbye."

"I understand. Goodbye, then, and I do hope you'll come back soon. I'll miss you, Number 6. You're my very favorite prisoner, you know. Give my regards to—"

Was he gone now? A regular rabbit, that fellow, when he had the chance.

"To my friend, Mr. Thorpe," Number 2 continued quietly, "if by any chance you should meet him in London."

Chapter Ten

At the Office

"I'm sorry, sir," the receptionist said, "but Mr Thorpe *is* engaged. If you care to wait until—"

"I've waited, already, three days."

"I understand there's a *crisis* somewhere." Having spoken this most magical of words, she thumped a fat fashion magazine on the glass desk, nodded at the neat rows of people behind the glass wall. "You can see that you're not the only one who's had to wait. The crisis—"

"There's always a crisis *somewhere*. Thorpe knows me. He knows I wouldn't bother him unless I had a crisis, too. For that matter, *you* know me."

Though she wavered at "crisis," she could resist any personal appeal. "If you say so, sir. I am only following Mr Thorpe's instructions, and his instructions were that he is not to be interrupted on any account."

"I won't be put off any longer by these rituals. I *must* speak to him!"

The receptionist caressed one of the photographs, as though his anger threatened not herself but the glossy image on the paper. Once or twice a year there would be one like this, one who simply would not leave her alone. As though there were anything *she* could do for them! It was the whole purpose of her being placed here, at this glass desk, overlooking the glass-walled waiting room, that she should signify to those who waited that nothing *could* be done for them, that they might stew there for days, weeks, months, and no attention be paid to them, no one would listen, that they were, in an official sense, invisible.

"He knows that, sir. A memo was taken to him on Wednesday afternoon, when you arrived, and again yesterday, and again this morning."

"If he knew I'm here, he'd see me."

Well, if he just refused to understand, then she would too! She started intently at the vibrant new nomad fashion mix, flurries of red fox about a wool tweed vest, a lace-stippled linen blouse, brown kidskin knickers, cataracts of heavy gold chain, and boots by Herbert Levine.

"I'll be back tomorrow morning."

"Just as you like, sir." She smiled with the go-native Nomad Look from Ultima II, a melange of terrific tawny shades: pinks, ambers, opals, amethysts. "Tomorrow is Saturday, however, and Mr Thorpe *golfs* on Saturdays."

"Then I'll see him at his club."

She nodded, clinking her necklaces, bobbing her curls, pressing the button that opened the glass wall. As he left (without a single pleasant word) she thought how, if it weren't for people like him, her job would have been almost perfectly ideal.

She buzzed the wall shut, and the pages of *Bazaar*

opened, like creamy petals, to swallow the frail butterfly of
her mind.

"I'm sorry, sir," said the clerk, as he entered the camera
shop, "but your projector isn't ready yet."

"It was promised for yesterday."

"We hadn't realized the problems involved, sir. If the
film were an ordinary size . . ."

"If I'd thought it would cost me all this trouble, I would
have done the work myself."

"And if *we'd* realized that, sir, we would have been
pleased to let you."

"When will I have it?"

"Tomorrow, sir. Our man is working on it now."

"Tomorrow is Saturday. You'll be closed."

"I'll be coming in just on your account, sir."

"Will you look at that, Jeremy?" the clerk said to the
man behind the curtain as soon as they were alone. "Have
you ever seen such *incivility*?"

"But Mr Plath, I told you I had his projector ready."

"You never seem to remember what I try to teach you
about *psychology*. Do you think he'd appreciate the effort
you've gone to if it were ready for him when it was
promised? Of course not. The more times he has to phone
up or come back, the more he'll realize how hard he's made
us work, and the more we can charge him for it."

"And you'll be coming in on a Saturday just for psychology, Mr Plath?"

"No, that was psychology too. The shop will open on
Monday at the usual hour."

"And won't the gentleman be angry?"

"Naturally, Jeremy. That's the *point*. When they're

furious, they'll pay any price just for the pleasure of throwing the bills on the counter and slamming the door. Why, once I got a customer to hit me starting off with no more than a simple black-and-white enlargement. He'd been coming here daily for three weeks. His attorney settled with mine for five hundred pounds—no, guineas it was. The best piece of work I've ever done. A triumph, Jeremy, an absolute triumph of psychology!"

"I'm sorry, sir," said the man behind the bar with a tactful frown. "You're quite correct in saying that this is Mr Thorpe's club, but—"

"*And* mine."

"Yes, sir, and yours, as you say. We've missed you recently. *But*, as I said, sir, this is Saturday. Mr Thorpe detests the course on Saturdays. It's so crowded, you know. Will you have another gin-and-tonic, sir?"

"I'm drinking Scotch."

"Of course, sir. You always drink Scotch, don't you? I don't know what's wrong with me today." As though to emphasize his malfunction, he dropped the glass he'd been drying for ten minutes into the sink: a starbust of crystal across the stainless steel.

The Muzak carpeted the air with *Humoresque*. He remembered having joined the club, but he could not remember his reasons.

"I'm sorry, sir," the old woman said with a pleased look, "but the Colonel is spending the weekend in the country."

"With whom, please? It's essential that I reach him at once."

"No doubt it is, sir. Everything that concerns the

Colonel is essential. But—" She jingled the ring of keys chained to her waist. "—I'm not at liberty . . ."

"Then who would be at liberty?"

The housekeeper shook her head, as though he'd asked a question that was at once meaningless and faintly immoral, an invitation to indulge in a physiologically impossible act. "*You* ought to know that better than *me*, sir."

With that careful flaw of grammar she had as much as slammed the door in his face. Servants, it implied, do not converse with gentlemen, ever. Then, realizing what she had implied, she did, in fact, slam the door in his face.

"I'm sorry, sir," said the operator, "but that number has been disconnected."

"In that case, perhaps you would do me a favor?" The receiver fizzed noncommittally. "Perhaps you would tell me *whose* number it was. Or the address, rather."

"What number did you say, sir?"

"COVentry-6121. Or COVent Garden. I'm not sure about the exchange."

"We're not allowed to give out that information over the phone, sir. I'm very sorry."

"Then why in hell did you ask the number?"

"I was *trying* to be helpful, sir," she answered aggrievedly.

He slammed the receiver into the cradle. His sixpence returned. He wanted to swear at someone, to their face, but there was only the telephone to swear at, an old black plastic telephone with halitosis, and you could see by its scars how often already it had been abused for the faults of its betters. Even so, he swore at it.

It couldn't be a plot. Not all of it. Not everywhere. Not

every one of them, the clerks in stores, the secretaries in offices, bartenders, servants, telephone operators.

It grew increasingly difficult to remember that the world had *always* been like this.

The glass wall slid open. He stepped through. Already, as the receptionist lifted up her smile to him, he heard the inevitable though still unspoken words, in the way an astronomer anticipates, before the sky darkens, the exact position of Saturn in the constellation of Scorpio.

"God morning, sir. Mr. Thorpe would like to see you right away."

"He . . . would?" (As though the planet had vanished!)

"Yes, sir. No, not that way, sir. He's upstairs, with Colonel Schjeldahl. Suite P, on 7. Do you know the way?"

"I can find it."

"You won't find it if you use *those* elevators, sir. They're for the public. Let me buzz a guard. He'll take you." She buzzed a guard. Before he'd been led away she remembered to ask: "Did you have a nice weekend, sir?" (That's the question you ask on Monday.)

He said, "Yes."

And even, "Thank you."

And, "Did you?"

"I had a *super* weekend, just super!"

How nice of him to have asked, she thought. *He's actually a lot of fun when you get to know him.*

"My dear fellow," said the Colonel, "before you go off the deep end, let us explain! In our position you would have done exactly the same thing. Wouldn't he, Dobbin?"

"Yes, Colonel," Thorpe replied, "he would."

"We want to help you, but we have a problem. Tell him our problem, Dobbin."

Thorpe tapped the mural world-map with an electric pointer, citing with each tap a city and an aspect of the problem. "You resign. You disappear. You return to us with a yarn that Hans Christian Andersen would reject for a fairytale."

The Colonel, who had some notion of who Hans Christian Andersen was, chuckled and made a note on his memo-pad so that when he described this scene later at his club he would remember his assistant's joke. A regular wasp of a fellow, this Thorpe!

"We must be sure," Thorpe continued, speaking quite slowly for the Colonel's benefit. "People do defect. An unhappy thought, but a fact of life. They defect, from one side to the other . . ."

"I also have a problem," he said. "I'm not sure which side runs this Village."

"And we're not sure that this Village even exists. It's highly improbable."

"I've shown you the pictures."

"Postcards and pencil sketches of a holiday resort."

"I have other documentation."

"We would like to see it," said the Colonel agreeably, having caught the drift again. "Wouldn't we, Dobbin?"

"Absolutely, Colonel! Anything he can produce even slightly more concrete. Names, for instance."

"As I explained, the residents are given numbers. One seldom knows, even, which are the prisoners and which are the guards. However, if I could look over photos of suspected defectors–covering, say, the last ten or even twenty years–I would probably recognize several faces."

"*That*, old man," Thorpe said, touching him with the pointer, "is exactly what we're afraid of."

"Then you won't help me?"

"The Colonel and I will carry the matter higher up. In the meantime, if you'd bring in this other documentation . . . ? Tomorrow, shall we say, at eleven?"

"After lunch would be better, Dobbin," the Colonel said. "I'm always tied up in the morning. Let's make it two o'clock. If we should need to get in touch with you before that, perhaps you'd tell my secretary where you can be reached."

"At the moment I'm between hotels. I'll be here tomorrow at two. I want to see Taggert then. The receptionist tells me he doesn't exist."

"Dobbin and I will be discussing this with him today."

"I would have preferred to be present when you talk to him. I have somewhat more confidence in his listening to me."

"A ladder," Thorpe said, "must be mounted rung by rung. Before you *retired*"–as he pronounced it, the word might have meant anything else except *retired*–"you could omit the lower rungs. In *those* days, it was you who stood between Taggert and me."

"You're enjoying this, aren't you, Thorpe?"

"Mildly, old man. Mildly."

The bedsheet was pinned across the drapes of the hotel room to form a screen. A small cigar smoked, forgotten, in the empty canister marked 14-LESB. The film was threaded into the modified Bell & Howell projector, for which he'd been charged thirty guineas above the list price. He had only to touch the switch and the past that had been stolen from him would unwind itself, at the rate of thirty-two frames per second, into his possession, restoring the shadow of a memory if not the memory itself.

Why this reluctance, then? Why did his hand hesitate? Wasn't the crucial thing, now, to recover what had been stolen? Until he did, his escape would be the hollowest kind of victory, for they would still hold his past hostage, in the prison files, like the leg a wolf leaves behind in the steel jaws of a trap.

He touched the machine that held his memory–and was shown:

A glass wall. Behind it, the people, waiting. Some thumbed through the familiar magazines with the same skilful inattention with which a pianist in a cocktail bar might whip through *Mood Indigo* for the tenth time in a single evening. Others, less practiced in patience, stared wistfully at the clockface above them, like spurned lovers who are still allowed to be *present* so long as they never declare their love.

The *same* people. He knew them. In this film they were a little younger, their clothes a bit fresher, their eyes not quite so dull–but the same. He had sat in that room with them hours at a time. He could not be mistaken.

Then, a medium close-up of Thorpe, dressed for golf. Behind him, indistinctly, the Colonel was poking about in the sandtrap next to the fourth hole.

"We must be sure," Thorpe said. "People do defect. An unhappy thought, but a fact of life. They defect, from one side to the other..."

The camera panned to his own face, zoomed in artfully to reveal the resentment that underlay the frustration, the stubbornness behind the resentment, and behind the stubbornness, the suspicion he had not permitted himself, consciously, either then or now.

"I have a problem too," he'd said. "I'm not certain which side runs the Village."

While the camera held its close-up on his face, the Colonel spoke: "A mutual problem."

"Which I'm going to solve."

"Quite," the Colonel said.

"If not here, then elsewhere."

There was no point in watching more of it. He switched it OFF, and in the darkness and the silence he caught the first whiff of the gas. The flickering.

He tried to stand amidst the sliding forms, on the warping carpet, above the roar.

The locked door was opening.

He knew that he had been captured long before he had escaped.

Chapter Eleven

On the Retina

"Where is he, Number 14? What is he doing?"

The woman in the white gown frowned, touching her closed eyelids gently with the tips of her fingers, touching then her temple where the white wires of the electrodes tangled in white hair. "Still at the gate, Number 2. Still at the gate."

"If you fed another image to him—" His voice entered the operating theater through six loudspeakers, an entire campanile of consonants and vowels, as though the disembodied speaker had converted his physical substance into pure sound.

"Until the fantasy begins to develop autonomously, there is no point in that. The subject's still in shock. I trust you observed the scene he made here, *despite* sedation. That he should dream at all in his present condition is astonishing to me. Let me remind you, Number 2, that rapport is difficult enough to maintain without these purpose-

less interruptions. Are you so possessed by the vice of conversation that you can't restrain your tongue's lust for half
an hour?"

"Number 14, if you think because you're wearing your
white smock that—"

"Each word you say, Number 2, is a wedge between his
mind and mine. Quiet now–he's moving! He's trying to . . .
get in."

"To get *in*!"

"Or out, I can't be sure. Such a vacant place. Just bars,
stretching up out of sight. Orangy-yellow light, no shadows. But a fine color sense. I think I'll *like* this one's
dreams. He's begun to subvocalize. Simple rhyming associ-
ations–they're not worth repeating. I think we can flash an
image to him now. Number 96, is the beam adjusted?"

The technical nurse gave one last tug at the subject's
head: clamped within the mold of tailored steel, it didn't
budge. She took a reading from the chrome Behemoth
positioned above his supine body. "Yes, Number 14, the
image should be clear as crystal."

"Number 28, I want just a silhouette, at ten milliseconds, until I've seen how long he holds the afterimage. I
suggest that we begin with a key, Number 2. It should take
him past those bars."

"I leave the matter in your fair white hands, Number 14.
Entirely."

"Number 28: a key."

In an adjacent room a young man sorted through a file
of slides, selected one, inserted it into the cybernetic idolon
he served, which coded the celluloid image into the mini-
mum series of retinal cues necessary to produce that
image. This code was then transmitted to the Behemoth (a

laser) positioned above the sedated subject. The infinitesimally brief image of a key was etched on to the retina of his left eye.

The woman winced as the wires twined in her white hair conveyed to her eyes the same dazzling image.

"*Ah*! Cut that to five milliseconds next time. It's far too bright. No, three. He's . . . How fast!"

"Yes?" the loudspeakers bellowed curiously. "*Well?*"

"I'm . . . he's in a church. The gate is an altar screen. I'm—"

"What of the key?"

Her laughter was warm, but such a little warmth was soon lost in the vast whiteness of this place, like a single germ struggling to survive in a vat of disinfectant. "What indeed! Tell me, Number 2, if the image of a key were blurred, what would it become?"

"Don't be a tease, woman! Just tell me what you . . . what *he* sees."

"An executioner's axe, and it's a whopping big one."

The priest mounted the pulpit, a rude wooden platform that creaked beneath his weight. He wore a simple alb over a black surplice and a black hood of imitation leather. Reaching the platform he stooped to pry the crescent-bladed axe from the wooden block. The unseen congregation spattered tepid applause. The priest lifted the axe, signaling for silence.

"Dearly beloved," he said, the orotund tones muffled by his hood, which had not been provided with a hole for the mouth, "and you especially, Number 6." Again applause, again the lifted axe.

"We are gathered here today to surrender, or render

unto seizers the things that are gauds. We must axe our-
selves who we really are, and let the sleeping doggerel that
is within us lie. This is the first stone, and upon this stone
we will spill our dirt, in order that these lies shall not have
been dyed with the blood of our veins."

He turned to the wispy, wrinkled, white-haired woman
next to him and inquired of her the name of this preacher.
Smiling, she pressed a senile finger to her withered lips, a
finger that resembled the numeral 1.

The preacher placed a large book upon the wooden
block and read to the congregation "The Crime of the
Ancient Mariner," chopping off the stanzas that displeased
him. Soon the pulpit was brimming with the lopped heads
of seagulls, but he continued to read the dismembered
poem, while the congregation reverently filed up the aisle to
receive, each, his own severed head.

"This is accomplishing nothing," Number 2 burst out
through his six speakers, after listening to the doctor chant
the first thirty stanzas of the "The Rime of the Ancient
Mariner." "We have learned only that at some point in his
schooldays he was required to memorize Coleridge's stupid
ballad, and that he now associates that memory with prisons. We must establish whether or not it was *he* who broke
into the archives and set that fire. That should be easy
enough to find out. Then, we shall explore his more interesting recesses."

"You had told me," the doctor said, "that there was no
doubt he'd done it. The two films taken from his file, one of
which was found in his possession in London. His fingerprints on everything. Any court could indict with evidence
that strong–*legally*!"

"That's why a doubt lingers. He isn't a bungler. It might well be that the film we found him watching was mailed to him, as he claims, in London. As for the fingerprints, they would have been available to any of us."

"Of us? Surely you don't think . . . ?"

"Everyone, including myself, would like to see certain of those records destroyed. Why did *you* first come to work for us, Number 14, eh? Not purely from your dedication to science. 3, likewise, would prefer to forget that unhappy incident in Poland. 4 might well wish for some final discontinuity with his 1952-model face. 6–his motives are different but even more compelling. 7? 7 is always whining that he wants to be back in London frying literature in a cork-lined cell."

"We both know, Number 2, that my brother is *incapable* of such derring-do. He's a dear boy, but *quite* incapable."

"Personally, I have a higher regard for the boy's capabilities, but that's not the issue."

"I would have thought you'd take more satisfaction in accusing *me*."

"Not accusing, Number 14–suspecting. None of us were continually before the cameras or with witnesses during that afternoon. Any of us *could* have used the tunnel to get to the Archives and back. Except 8, of course. He was in *your* care at the time, wasn't he. But 9, 10, 11, 12, 13, any of *them*, in any combination."

"It all sounds very baroque to me."

"Rococo, if you like. It isn't *my* idea in any case–it's Number 1's."

For the first time during this exchange, she opened her eyes: they were of different colors, one milky blue, one hazel-brown. "Damn!" She closed them quickly, covered her face with her hands. The high pale brow furrowed with concentration.

"Did you lose rapport?" Number 2 asked anxiously.

"No I'm still . . . the priest is still chopping up seagulls."

"And the vocal?"

"This one's a strong subvocalizer, so that's no problem. I do wish you wouldn't say things to startle me like that. I *could* have lost touch. Now, what image do you suggest in order to lead him back to the scene of the crime?"

"Why not a photograph of the room?"

"Too complicated. The laser would burn his eyeballs out before enough identifying detail could be established. It has to be something readily gestalted."

"Could you suggest a descent down a spiral staircase?"

"Number 28," she called out, "do we have anything like that?"

"Just regular staircases," the young man replied from the next room. "There's a code classified as 'Vertigo.' Would that do?"

"Possibly. Space out the cues, and it should be almost the same sensation."

"Right."

Number 14 gasped. "*Slower*! It's—Oh! oh, this is awful, I can't—Slower!"

"If I space the cues out much more," he complained, "the program will run to five minutes before it's completed."

"Then cancel it. The resemblance to a stairway of any kind is nil."

After a long pause Number 2 asked: "Where is he? In the crypt?"

"Not there, no. I don't recognize the place. We'll just have to let him make his way around, until I can tell. We can't feed more cues to him for five minutes at least. That 'Vertigo' sequence was murderous. Number 28, make a note to modify the code for 'Vertigo.' Strange ... I'd swear I've seen a place exactly like this, but for the life of me ..."

He was in hell. The parks were planted with beds of tulips and marigolds. Muzak played in the busy streets. It was a holiday. CLOSED signs hung in all the windows. The signs in the grass said SMILE.

He asked the taxi driver what the place was called, but the taxi driver said he wasn't allowed to go there. Like all the other damned souls, the driver was very small, almost a miniature.

The old woman he had sat next to in church got in the back seat and sat next to him in the taxi.

"Are you going to vote today?" she asked, smiling.

"Who is there to vote for?" A rhetorical question.

She tisked. "There's always Someone to vote for, Number 6. Here—" She dug into her purse and took out a large gilt button, which she pinned to the lapel of his jacket. It said:

GUILT

"That's some kind of progress anyhow," Number 2 grumbled. "It shows that his attitude is maturing."

"No, wait—She's getting out. He took the button off the minute she was gone, put it in the ashtray. He wore it from courtesy rather than conviction. Now he's getting out. There's a large hill. And there's Rover. This must have something to do with his escape. Now he's pushing Rover up the hill."

"An allusion to Sisyphus, my dear. Number 6 has a classical education."

"Rover's talking to him. Do you want to hear what—"

"Of course, woman! It isn't *Rover* talking to him, it's *me*. He's dreaming about *me!*"

She let the patient's unspoken words, the dream's faint resonance in his larynx, be amplified by her own mouth, shaped by her own lips. The voice Number 2 heard was neither hers nor his, but theirs together:

> "But tell me, tell me! speak again,
> Thy soft response renewing—
> What makes that ship drive on so fast?
> What is the ocean doing?"

"Oh hell, hell, hell, hell, hell, hell," the six loudspeakers chorused. But Number 2 knew better than to interrupt again, so, while Sisyphus/6 struggled at his task and the Ancient Mariner jingled interminably toward redemption, he waited, daydreaming of his own hells, the ones he had already made, the better hells to come.

Hell is filled with The Sound of Music. *Forlornly, he pushes the great beige stone up the hill; forlornly, it rolls down again. How many times? How many more? Forlornly, up the hill; forlornly down. He has read this myth, he knows the story, but he was caught within the role and his contract required him to stay with the show for its entire run, and already it was threatening the record set by* The Moustrap.

* * *

"No, Number 2, the only vocal I get now is just those songs. I get the impression that he's thinking too, but I don't get a glimmer what about."

"Nonsense, nobody *thinks* in their dreams! That's the wonderful thing about the id, that it doesn't have to think. But I shouldn't lecture you in your own speciality. While you were warbling, I thought of an image certain to prove whether or not he was down there. The one film of him that had been put on the bonfire concerned an earlier contretemps with a double we provided for his amusement way back when. What was left on the reel showed that it was reversed, as though it had recently been played through quickly and not rewound. Let's flash the image of his own face on to his retina. Surely, if he saw that film, there'll be some indication in his dream."

"There's one drawback in that. I've done the same thing with other subjects, usually in the routine course of charting libidinal structures. Seeing oneself tends to bring one nearer consciousness, especially when there is a strong narcissistic component."

"If he starts to rise to the surface, we can drag him back under with a big heavy archetype."

"All right. Let's have a photograph of Number 6."

"Here it is," Number 28 called into the amphitheater.

"28, you oaf! That was a profile! I wanted him full-face. No one ever sees himself in *profile*. Damn! It's too late."

Outnumbered, he continued to struggle. The guards forced him down on the operating table. The surgeon appeared, all in white. Even her hair, though she was no older than

himself, was white, spun glass, luminous. Though of differ-
ent colors, her two eyes showed a distinct resemblance one
to the other. In her own analytical way, she seemed to be
admiring him.

"Number 28, hand me the new identity, please."

The young man handed the surgeon a wide, somewhat
Slavic face. She examined the profile, touched the mus-
tache tentatively, ran a comb through the dark hair, chang-
ing the part from the right to the left.

"Hold still, please, Number 6. This won't hurt."

She grafted the face to his, tugging at the seams when
she had finished to make certain it would not come off
under pressure.

"Excellent! Now bring me that other body, Number 28,
the one from the freezer. Once we've locked him in that,
he'll be no trouble at all. There's no sturdier cage than a
hundredweight or two of good solid flesh."

"This other face, what does it look like, Number 14?"

"Like his, of course."

"In the film, at one point, he was shown with a mustache and his hair darkened. If the face in the dream—"

"No, Number 2. The new face is *exactly* the same." (And,
she added with silent spite, *you* can go to hell. Her lie was
not a matter of protecting the subject so much as it was a
way of getting at *him*.)

The loudspeakers soughed a sigh. "Of course, that
doesn't prove it *wasn't* Number 6."

"Unfortunately, though, it won't convince Number 1
that it couldn't have been one of us. For my own part, I'm
convinced it was 6. Shall we keep trying?"

"How much time have we left?"

"Ten minutes at most. Beyond that there's a danger of personality disintegration–for either of us or both. Also a possibility of reversal, which is harmless but a waste of time. That is, if I try to channel the dream too often where I want it to go, he may start dreaming *my* dream. Or else–I'm not sure just how it does happen–I lose an objective sense of what his dream is about, like critics who find their own theories in everyone else's books."

"I can see you're under a strain, Number 14. You never start to lecture me until you're tired. So, with the time left, I'd like–Oh, what is he doing now, by the way? Still strapped down?"

"In effect. He seems to regard the second body as a kind of straitjacket."

(*The way he stares at me,* she thought. *I wish he wouldn't.*)

"We must learn something about the interval he spent away from us. Not his little jaunt last week to London, but the longer absence when he was not observed. Once we know who was involved in his brainwashing, we'll have a fair idea of what techniques were used. I suggest, therefore, that you begin with the photograph of Number 41."

Liora!

He tried to approach her, but though the straps had been removed, his imprisoning flesh was adamantine, unyielding.

He tried to speak, but his mouth would not form the syllables of her name.

Her name–Liora. And her eyes.

Her eyes!

* * *

"What fantasies now, eh?" If loudspeakers could wink . . .

"Nothing."

"Nothing? But I thought they were in love!"

"Wait. Her eyes—"

"Only her *eyes*?"

"—are glowing. The strangest thing."

"That's as good as nothing. I think you should chart *his* libidinal structure."

"Incredibly, incredibly bright. I—I—Oh, it's—"

"Try and get a *real* response out of the lout, Number 14. Let's flash him a weapon, or something *positive*."

"So bright. My God, Number 2—it's beautiful! I've never seen a thing so beautiful. And he's—Why does she—"

She screamed.

"Number 14?"

She had fainted. As she slumped forward, the electrodes tore loose from her temples, unravelled from the white hair, and at the same moment, her patient woke smiling amid the collapse of his dream.

PART III

NUMBER GAMES

"Thus, albeit straitly confined in a small enough cage, Fabrizio led a fully occupied life; it was entirely devoted to seeking the solution of this important problem: 'Does she love me?' The result of thousands of observations, incessantly repeated, but also incessantly subjected to doubt, was as follows: 'All her deliberate gestures say no, but what is involuntarily in the movement of her eyes seems to admit that she is forming an affection for me.'"

Stendhal, *The Charterhouse of Parma*

Chapter Twelve

The Nomination Committee

The fat woman ascended from the sofa, like a giant squid rising out of the sea, in a froth of pink chiffon. "May we congratulate you," she burbled, "on your *swift* recovery?" His hand still on the knob, he stared with glum astonishment at the crowd assembled in his living room. Three . . . four . . .

Seven of them.

"Budgie, my dear," said the fat man, also rising (the teak creaked relief), "*shouldn't* we apologize first? We have, you know, rather invited ourselves."

"But, dear darling sweet, it would hardly have been a *surprise* if *he'd* invited us!" She smiled with a Gargantuan coquettishness, inviting him to share her amusement at dear darling sweet's inanity.

"You should, at the very least then, *introduce* us." He shrugged bloated shoulders, as though to say: *Our Budgie is incorrigible, but we must love her just the same.*

"I was just *about* to, my pigeon, before you interrupted. Be assured, Number 6," she said, her hand fluttering forward to roost on his, clenched about the doorknob, "that we would never have taken this liberty"—she tittered, as though, she had risked a slightly off-colored remark—"without Number 14's assurance—"

The doctor nodded to him with the very smallest smile. Not half an hour ago, he had left her in her ceremonial white smock at the hospital. Now she wore a summer dress of silky pastel flowers. A cluster of fresh-cut roses was pinned to the white wide-brimmed straw hat that framed the whiter hair.

"—that you would be *delighted*—"

"Thrilled!" the pigeon added, his head bobbing up and down excitedly.

"—by the news we've brought you."

"The offer, so to speak," the pigeon explained. "The opportunity."

"I am, or rather I have been, the Mayoress of this Village, and *this* is my husband."

The pigeon blushed to have his distinction so publicly proclaimed. "Number 34," he murmured modestly.

"Yes," the ex-Mayoress continued, "he is Number 34 and now I have no other wish *myself* than to become, once more, Number 33, a private citizen, a mere equine among equines. Your other guests constitute, with us, the Nomination Committee in its entirety. You are already acquainted with Number 14."

"Number 6 and I are almost old friends by now," the doctor said.

"Have you met her brother too? Number 7, one of our youngest citizens, but not by any means the least."

The young man who bounded forward to shake his hand looked to be in his mid-twenties. If her brother, then distinctly a kid brother. He shared the doctor's idiosyncratic good looks: the fine hair was cut down to a nap of blond cornsilk; lively eyes of a stark, ingenuous blue; a wide, dimpled chin; a wide, dimpling smile; a nose just pleasantly out of plumb; clothes of calculating modesty.

"I've looked forward so much to meeting you, sir," he said, earnestly, gripping his hand with convulsive strength. "My sister's always talking about you. Everybody talks about you. I think—"

Then, stage-struck, words failed. He smiled dismally at imagined spotlights and dropped his hand. The blue eyes stared at the splendid, unobtrusive, hand-sewn cordovans from Maxwell's, Dover Street.

The fat man led Number 7 back to stand beside his sister, who took the dangling, defeated hand fondly between hers.

"We're all very *fond* of Number 7," the fat woman confided loudly, "but he does have an enormous sensibility sometimes. It only lasts a moment, and then he'll be himself again, if we just ignore him. Now, let me see, who's left? Do you know Number 83?"

The man indicated stood apart from the other Committee members, slouched against the damask curtains of the false window, waiting to be photographed. His arm was in a bright Madras sling.

"I ran into Number 6 at the railway station the day he arrived—but we were never formally introduced."

"Well, well," the pigeon cooed, "numbers aren't that important, are they? With some of my best friends I can't remember their numbers from one minute to the next."

The fat woman shrieked agreement. The pigeon,

rewarded, tried to repeat his success. "I'll lay odds that old Granny here doesn't even know her own number. "I'm sure that none of *us* do, anyhow."

Granny (there could be no doubt which one of them was "Granny") gave a dry chuckle. Sitting all folded up on one of the Chippendale chairs, she seemed more than ever to be a greeting card come, just barely and for only a little while, to life.

"Pigeon-poo," the ex-Mayoress chided, "what a *terrible* truth for you to say! Of course she knows her number. We all do. She's . . . she's . . ."

"Number 18," said Number 7.

"Number 42," said Number 14.

"Number *60*," said the fat woman, resolving their discord with a sum. Isn't that so, Granny dear?"

"Yes, thank you," said the old woman. "With a wee bit of milk, please, and one lump of sugar."

The pigeon sniggered. The fat woman sighed. She patted the aged hands with the expert condescension of a Practical Nurse. "In just a minute, Granny. We haven't *actually* been invited to stay."

He remained grimly silent. It was clear now why he'd been released from the hospital while he was still reeling from the sodium pentathol.

The pigeon pouted his lips and rolled his eyes in a dumb-show of social distress, as though his wife had just spilled the imaginary cup of tea on the Sirhaz carpet.

"We call her Granny, you see," the ex-Mayoress twittered on imperturbably, "because she's been here in the Village longer than any of the rest of us can remember. And she's *such* a darling that you can't help feeling that she *is* your grandmother. Especially since there is such, how would I put it—" The face frowned itself into a cluster of pink grapes.

"A scarcity," the doctor suggested, with a squeeze of her brother's hand, "of more authentic family relationships?"

"Ah, doctor, you are blunt, blunt, but your mind cuts like a knife! That's just what was never so well expressed. Now, is that all of us?"

"Me?" asked the seventh committee member, pressing his Homburg into his lap.

"Oh yes, last but not—" She coughed. "Number 98. If you've been into the Stationer's, Number 6, you might remember him." (Or, her tone implied, you might not.)

The Stationer's clerk rose from his chair and approached his unwilling host. "We've had the pleasure, that is to say, I've had it, when this gentleman . . . The uh, sketchpad, if you . . . ?"

He lifted his hand meekly, not so much offering it to be shaken as to question its suitability for that purpose, or any other. His host did nothing to relieve him of the responsibility for this decision, and he retired, with his questionable hand, to the chair, where his Homburg was able to offer him some degree of reassurance.

"There now!" the fat woman said contentedly. "We're all *friends*."

The Nomination Committee looked at him, each member smiling his or her characteristic smile, each refusing to acknowledge the obvious message of his determined silence and the door he held wide open.

At last he conceded defeat: "In that case, would you do me the courtesy of explaining your friendly visit?"

"*You* tell him, Budgie," Number 34 insisted.

"It's hardly for *me* to do that! *You* tell him, pigeon."

"But I can't! Don't you remember–I'm on the *Election* Committee. It wouldn't do!"

Finally it was Number 14 who, with no attempt to conceal her amused disdain for the idea, broke the news to him: "The Nomination Committee has decided to nominate you, Number 6, to succeed Number 33 as Mayor of the Village."

"The Nomination Committee would have saved themselves a lot of trouble if they'd asked me first. I refuse to be considered."

"Didn't I tell you, Budgie," the pigeon burst out angrily. "Didn't I *predict*?"

"Your refusal doesn't affect the nominating procedures, I'm afraid. In fact, the ballots are already printed, and the election is tomorrow."

"My thanks, then, for having informed me. Now, I suppose, you must be anxious to fly away and tell the other candidates the same good news."

"There are no other candidates, Number 6. You were our unanimous choice."

"Unanimous," they murmured in chorus. Even Granny's lips seemed to approximate the right syllables.

"So," the fat woman said, "in effect, you are already our new Mayor. May I be the first to offer you my sincere congratulations?"

"All right then, elect me Mayor. Proclaim me president, proconsul, anything you like. But don't expect me to act my part in the farce."

"As for that," the doctor said, "you needn't worry. The Mayor has no duties whatever."

The ex-Mayoress puffed up indignantly, and the pigeon rallied to her defense: "I'm amazed at you, Number 14–to say such a thing! Why, the Mayor of this Village has *unbe-lievable* duties!"

"*Utterly* unbelievable," she echoed. "Not to *mention* all the paper-work involved."

Granny's hands, which till now had been resting in her lap emblematic of the peace that passeth understanding, seemed to have sensed (independently of her face, which still wore the same serene smile) the discord growing about them, for they were wandering in agitation all about the crepe of her dress, plucking at folds and tugging at buttons.

It was Number 98, the Stationer's clerk, who first noticed these symptoms of distress. He rushed across the room and knelt beside the old woman, trying to soothe the troubled hands, whispering to them and petting them.

He looked up imploringly at his host. "She really should have a cup of tea, sir. All this dissension, it's bad for..." One of the hands escaped from him, grabbed for his ear. "...her heart!"

"Very well," he said. "We don't want to make more work for Number 14. Darjeeling or Earl Gray?"

"Earl Gray. But don't you trouble yourself, sir–I can make it. It will only take me a...a..." He looked for the word on the carpet.

"An *hour* at the very most," Number 14 said, helpfully. "And I'll take lemon with mine, if you have one that's fresh."

The pigeon and his wife plumped down with one accord on to the brave little sofa. "Budgie would prefer cream to milk," he called out to Number 98, who had run into the kitchen.

"And my little pigeon likes *his* just as sweet as sweet can be, doesn't he?"

Her little pigeon gave his big Budgie a little peck.

"Now, Number 6," the doctor said, tapping a sharp almond nail on the arm of the Chippendale the clerk had vacated, "why don't you sit down and make yourself at home?"

"I hope you don't mind my staying on this late," said the doctor's younger brother, helping himself to another Scotch. "But it was important I speak to you *alone*. What time is it, by the way?"

"Mm! What? Oh, yes." He opened his eyes, studied his unwound watch. "Nearly six. P.M., that is."

Every surface of the room was covered with dirty cups and saucers, plates of biscuits, ashtrays, and glasses half full of watery liquor.

"They all just insisted on staying. I was getting desperate," Number 7 said.

"They did, yes, and so was I. When you say that we're alone, though, you forget—" He gestured to the corner where the numberless old woman, noticed, twinkled benignly and chinked cup against saucer, as though to say: What a very *nice* party!

"Oh, but that's just Grandmother Bug. No one worries about *her*."

"Bug? Isn't that unkind?"

"It doesn't bother *her*! does it, Granny?" He flashed a triply-dimpled smile at the old woman, and she gave another chink of recognition: What a fine time we're *all* having!

"There's a theory, I don't say that I believe it, that she isn't altogether, how do you say, *alive*. Just a kind of machine. A mechanical person, like in *The Tales of Hoff-*

mann. To my mind, extreme senility amounts to the same thing–one is reduced to the condition of a machine. Of course, age only makes it more obvious."

"Makes what more obvious? Excuse me, I was dozing."

"I mean, with the sort of thing my sister does at the hospital you don't need to make *machines* to do that sort of thing."

"What sort of thing?"

"Well, anything. In her case, bugging. Which is why it makes no difference if Granny stays on. This cottage must be bugged in any case. Do you have access to the floor above this?"

"No."

"That's the standard design. There should be four cameras here in the living room–I see one of them just above the mirror–and three in the kitchen, four again in the bedroom, and one in the W.C."

"Two."

"Ah, you have a shower. I only have a tub."

Once more the young man braked to a sudden silence. Stirring his drink morosely, he resumed at a safer speed. "You'll probably think this is ridiculous, but I felt I had to tell you that I admire what you've been doing. Terribly much." As though recoiling from his own confession, or perhaps simply unaccustomed to this much Scotch, he collapsed on to a Chippendale.

"What have I been doing?"

"Your escape! You don't think anyone is taken in by the story that you spent this whole week in the hospital–? My sister told me all the details. *She* was terribly impressed too. We both think you're wonderful. Do you . . . I mean, my sister, does she . . . ?"

She tried to brainwash me, if that's what you're getting at."

"Oh, no! I mean, of course she did, that's her *job*, but she didn't do anything like what she *might* have. You have a very strong ego structure."

"Thank you."

"It's a fact. She says it's almost impregnable. But what I meant to say, before, was—are you . . . fond of her?"

He laughed, and Grandmother Bug laughed with him, a little uncertainly, for she'd been caught unawares. If they were telling jokes now, she would have to pay closer attention.

One could not tell if the young man's sigh was one of relief or disappointment.

"Perhaps you think that she's . . . cold? Women doctors generally give the wrong impression that way, you know. Even before she was brought here, it was always painful for me to see how people reacted to her. Actually, she's a very *warm* person."

"One of the warmest in the Village, I've no doubt."

"Oh, but you can't blame her for being here, anymore than you can blame yourself. We're all *victims*, you know. She was blackmailed into coming. Three months after she arrived, they got to me. I was *kidnaped!* It was the most exciting thing that ever happened to me."

"What do you do for them?"

"Me? I've never done anything for anyone, except keep them company. My sister says I'm a dilettante, but that makes it sound more *professional* that it really is. I imagine they thought it would improve her morale if I were around. I imagine it has. We've been awfully close to each other since we were this big." His fingers measured a smallish embryo. "Also, I write. Poetry." He made it sound like one of the least fashionable diseases. "But then anyone who doesn't have anything better to do *writes*. Do you write? No, of course not, not *you*. That's just why I admire you so, because you do do things. And what I want to suggest is–well, you'll probably think this is absurd–"

"That's beside the point."

"I'd like, if you'd let me, to *help* you."

"To help me do what?"

"To escape, obviously. I mean, when one is in prison, isn't that what a person like yourself *ought* to do?"

"You consider yourself a likely ally?"

"This time it was Number 7's turn to laugh, and again Grandmother Bug was taken by surprise. These two certainly did have the strangest way of telling jokes.

The laughter expired bubbling into the Scotch. "Don't, please take offense, Number 6, but it wasn't at all the sort of response I would have expected from *you*. I mean, it was almost, if you'll excuse my saying so, naive. The whole point of the way this place is organized is so that you can never trust anyone. Any of us could be one of *them*. You could be, for all I know, and my sister could be too."

"Your sister is."

"Not at root. At root she's on our side."

"Then isn't it unwise of you to say so?"

"Not if they already suspect it themselves. Besides, if she is one of them, then she's all the more valuable to them if she were to seem, in a way, not to be. That's why *you* would make such a splendid agent for their cause, because you appear to be such a thorough-going rebel. It's like psychoanalysis that way–if a thing is true, then its opposite is also true–or if it isn't, it's at least much more probable.

You're making such faces, Number 6, but I'm only saying what everyone in the Village takes for granted, the By-Laws, as it were. I'm surprised you hadn't figured all that out yourself. Or are you only annoyed at the rest of us for having figured it out too? It's not that we're all such sly foxes–but what else is there to *think* about here? In any case, the upshot of it is that I'm just as likely a candidate to be of service to you as anyone. I might, of course, be Number 1 himself, incognito–" He chuckled self-deprecatingly.

Grandmother Bug, recognizing her cue and having prepared herself, produced her very best laugh, a soprano cackling that modulated into helpless tears, a shaking head, and a dying fall of "Lord! O Lordie! Lord!"

"Or I might be, as I'd like you to believe, perfectly sincere in making the offer. The only way you'll ever know is to try me. You're shuffling your feet. You want me to leave now, don't you?"

"Hospitality has limits, and with that glass you've pretty well exhausted them. Unless you want to switch to gin. Also, I don't think Granny ought to be sent home without an escort."

"I'm going right this minute. There's just one last thing, which may not seem that important to you, though it is to me. Do you have any idea why you should have been given that number? Why 6?"

"I never thought to question it. Six of one, half a dozen of the other."

"You think it's that simple? *We're* all inclined to think there's some significance, perhaps even a crucial one, in our numbers. For instance, Number 1 and Number 2 are just what one would expect of a 1 and a 2."

"I wouldn't know. I've never seen or heard the first, and I know the second only through the media, so to speak."

"But ought not a Number 1, if he wants to play God, preserve something like God's silence and invisibility? One is an *absolute* idea, and reality never measures up to absolutes. As for Number 2, you'll probably be granted an audience soon enough. Dictators are usually queasy about exposing themselves to the dictated. Understandably."

"Have you met him? Off the screen, that is."

" 'Met' would be too strong a word. I've *seen* him. Which is more than my sister can claim. They're not friends, but I don't hold that against him. My sister is hard to get to know. But to return to my theory: take her number as a for-instance. She's Number 14, which is twice seven. And *I'm* Number 7!"

"Are you twins?"

"No, but there are nearly seven years between us."

"And seven deadly sins."

"And *sixth* columns. I know all this symbolism is silly, but I do have the feeling that there must be some sort of what would you call it? Not link."

"Affinity?"

"Yes! An affinity between us, seeing that you're Number 6 and I'm Number 7. At least it's true of me and Number 8. We're tremendous friends. At least we were."

"What happened? Did you try and help him escape?"

"Oh no! 8 was very much the company man. What happened is he went around the twist. Paranoia, *soaring* paranoia. It's the people who are loyalist to the Village who are the most susceptible. They begin to think everyone is betraying the cause but themselves. And Number 1, of course-no one ever doubts *his* loyalty. Which is another good reason he should be invisible. No one doubts what he can't see."

"But they do doubt Number 2's loyalty?"

"Especially his."

"Speak of the devil," said a voice from behind the damask curtains, "and I appear."

Grandmother Bug crumbled out of her chair with a nervous squeak, dropping cup and saucer on the carpet. The cold untasted tea formed a dark oval that overlapped the interlocking pears.

"We'd better be going now," Number 7 shouted, wrestling the old woman back to her feet. "It's how late I hadn't realized and—"

"It was a pleasure," he said, opening the door for them.

"The pleasure was mine," Grandmother Bug chirruped, remembering her party manners. "I don't know *when* I've had such a lovely little pleasure." Her hand fluttered about the high collar of her dress, in search of the button of the coat she had not worn these last thirty years.

Number 7 pulled her out the door roughly. "We *both* don't know," he said to the closing door. "And thanks a lot."

He faced the drawn drapes which were speckled by the cold flickering light of the television.

"Thank you, Number 2. You accomplished that very economically. I hope you're not looking for company, too."

"No. I thought I'd take the opportunity to offer you my congratulations on your new honor. Congratulations! And to tell you that your first mayoral duty should arrive at your doorstep any minute."

"It can sleep there if it wishes, but it won't be let in. I

promised the voters that I'd never perform the duties of my office, and one must keep faith with the electorate."

"That would be unkind. You see, this is her first day out in the Village, and she's still extremely disorientated. It's the Mayor who explains to newcomers our little customs and mores."

"She? Who?"

"Number 41. But I see—"

The doorbell rang.

"—that she's arrived. So I'll leave the two of you alone. Do try and be some comfort to her, Number 6. The poor thing doesn't know where to turn at this point." The faint glow faded behind the damask.

He went to the door. Even now, despite the suspicion Number 2 had awakened (the hope, as well?), he might have bolted it. If there had been a bolt.

He opened the door.

"Liora!"

She took a step backward, staring at him, with that ill-feigned unconcern one pays to lunatics and freaks.

"Pardon me, but I was told that this was the residence of the Mayor. Are you ..." She looked at the scrap of paper in her hand. "... Number 6?"

Chapter Thirteen

Number 41

He twisted the dial its clockwise limit; the living room became a glare of incandescence in which they examined each other–he to confirm that this was indeed Liora, she as though she were encountering for the first time and without protection the chief suspect in a notorious murder trial, in the very room where the corpse had been discovered.

She was, unquestionably, Liora. Her appearance had not been modified even by such little changes of emphasis as one expects to encounter in a woman of fashion after a two-months' absence. The brown suit was familiar to him, the bracelet disguising a watch, the emerald pendant. Her modish Sassoon haircut had grown out to an unmodish length, and he remembered her telling him, during their dinner at the Connaught, that she'd decided to let it grow long again. By all the signatures of identity–her carriage, her speech, the small transitions between two almost identical expressions–she declared herself to be Liora.

"Do you find the light better in here?" he asked.

"The implication being that I should recognize you? I don't, of course, but I expect you'll want to carry on with whatever little masque you've gotten up for the occasion."

Even that "gotten" was hers, a declaration of her origins as convincing as any stamped on a passport. (In her case, he recalled, even more convincing, for she had traveled usually as a citizen of a long-defunct banana republic.)

"Is this a game, Liora, and if so whose side have you taken? Or am I being punished for having declined your recentest proposal?"

"Shouldn't you offer me a seat before you open the script? Evidently, the plot is elaborate. And I *am* tired, as you know."

"By all means, sit where you like. I'm sorry I can't offer you a Scotch. The last two members of the committee that was here to inform me of my mayoralty left just before you arrived. You can see from the debris that they were thorough." He lifted the empty green bottle to the light.

"I never drink Scotch."

"There's gin."

"Gin-and-ginger. Thank you."

"When I was in London last week," he said, uncapping a Schweppes, "I tried to call you. Your line had been disconnected. A month before that I reached a bookshop when I dialed the number. Where have you been this month?"

"So, for all your mummery, this is only to be *another* interrogation?"

He handed the drink to her. "You think I'm one of them?"

"The alternative would seem to be that *I* am. Or that I'm unhinged."

He considered other possibilities.

"Or," he added after a long pause, "that I am. Unhinged, that is. They do tamper with people's heads."

"If it's to be this complicated, I shall need pencil and paper to keep it all straight. Let us, for the sake of proper exposition, define our presumptive identities. First, my name is not Liora, it's Lorna. I've been told that so long as I'm detained here that I'm to answer to the name of Number 41, though if you care to tell me now that I'm another number entirely I won't protest that. I was abducted on the seventh of July, from my flat in Bayswater. It was done with something like ether, I suppose, unless there's some more contemporary drug that accomplishes the same thing. I don't know how long I was kept unconscious. I woke in the hospital here, feeling unaccountably weak and quite accountably confused. At first I thought I'd had an accident. I've always been terrified that some day I'd injure my brain. A woman doctor with unmatched eyes ran me through an interminable battery of tests. I cooperated for some time, since the tests gave me a sense of security, of being undamaged. Then the hospital staff became inquisitive about things that ought not to interest hospitals, and I stopped cooperating. Some imbecile of a male nurse released me this morning. Of course I immediately tried to get out of the Village. When it had been demonstrated that one does not *leave* this Village, that one must *escape* from it, I went to the local restaurant and enjoyed the view from the Tarpeian Rock. The imbecile from the hospital found me there and gave me a slip of paper with your name–your number, rather–and a sketch of how I was to find your house. And there you have it, everything I know. Now lay down *your* cards and let's see if you have a canasta."

"Do you know the Connaught in London?"

"A hotel?"

"And a restaurant. Near the American Embassy. You're still an American, aren't you, in your new identity?"

"It's a relief to know you're not going to try and persuade me I'm actually Turkish. As for the Connaught, I'm certain I've never done more than walk past it, if that. The only hotel I know in London is the Savoy, and that was ages ago."

"Then let me begin my story by telling you about the dinner we ate at the Connaught on the evening of June 6th."

"And then," she said, ending his tale for him, "the doorbell rang, and it was me, the girl of your dreams."

"Was it? I'm still trying to decide. You'll admit that my story is no more improbable than yours?"

"Only somewhat more ornamented. It remains, however, a story. You, on your side of the mirror, will claim the same thing. It was a long way to go to reach the same impasse. Again we see that either I am lying or you are lying."

"Or neither," he added.

"Or we are both Cretans, but we can't consider that possibility with any pretense to consistency, though dramatically it would be the most appealing."

"If I'm lying, it would mean that you're of interest to our jailers on your own account. Are you?"

"Hopefully, I'm interesting to all kinds of people. Contrariwise, if I'm lying, my arrival would be part of the general plot against your sanity, yes?"

"Yes. And if neither of us is lying, it's a plot against both our sanities."

"It's a nice theory," she said, if only on account of all

the *machinery* that would have to be involved. If one of us is lying, then we must act out a simple melodrama of innocence pitted against iniquity. While, if we're both perfectly *sincere* in contradicting each other, then it's a matter of *our* much larger innocence and *their* enormous iniquity. There would be ambiguities, in every glance and clues buried in every commonplace. So if we're to continue in our roles, stagecraft as well as etiquette seems to demand that we assume *that* to be the case. Do you agree?"

"For the time being."

"So it stands thus–that we both think we're telling the truth. Now, Mr. Pirandello, resolve that."

"Either I did know you and you are Liora, or I didn't and you aren't. If the second case obtains, then I've been brainwashed into thinking otherwise, and the brainwashing would have to have been done *before* I was brought here, since I tried to call you within hours of my arrival."

"Possibly while those other memories were being amputated, these were being grafted on."

"Possibly," he said. "But I'm inclined to believe that it wasn't anyone connected with the Village who arranged my amnesia. If they had, why would they be bothering with me now? They'd have what they wanted."

"Perhaps they want you to work for them." A tinselly laugh underlined her irony.

"Then why set me loose after they'd ordered my brain to their liking? Simply so *we* could dine at the Connaught?"

"Let's grant that Occam's razor won't slice that, though we're already *miles* from the simplest solution. You think we must posit another set of *theys* to account for your amnesia?"

"I think so. If there is someone who is desperate to

obtain information, there must also be someone equally desperate to keep it to themselves. Couldn't you imagine your own people doing the same thing, if they thought there was a likelihood of your telling their secrets to, for instance, our jailers?"

"I can imagine it all too easily. So, I'll allow you both sets of *theys*. The problem then arises, why would these other *theys* want to make you believe you knew me? After all, it was these *theys*, here in the Village, who have arranged our meeting."

"And it's a problem I have no solution for. Unless both *theys* have interlocking Boards of Directors."

"The mind boggles."

"That's what they're hoping, Liora-that the mind will boggle."

"Lorna, please."

"There's one other reason why I don't think the manu-facturers of my amnesia could also be the engineers of the presumed 'false memory'-and that is the clear recollection I have of our dinner. They could have inserted false memo-ries into our past, but how could they have dibbled with my future? That dinner took place *after* they'd done their work, and immediately after the dinner I set off from Paddington. The next morning-or to be precise, the next time I woke-I was here."

"This dinner that you harp on-just how distinctly *do* you recall it? Most of the dinners in *my* memory are jum-bled into one big stewpot of leftover scraps."

"I remember what the waiter looked like, the ring on his hand, the wax on his mustache. It was you, in fact, who pointed out those two details. I remember the bouquet on our table, a single rose in a silver vase. I remember how you looked and things you said. I remember the *taste* of each dish, the wines that accompanied each course. With the bisque we had a Solera, Verdalho Madeira, 1872. With the salmon, Coindreu—"

"I'm certain if I *had* had dinner with you and you'd played the wine-snob so grossly, I would have laughed in a most memorable way."

"My snobbery took me in the other direction: I didn't *mention* the wines then. But, as the dinner set me back almost fifty pounds, I do recall the vintages quite well."

"It strikes me that this scene is *unnaturally* clear. Especially since the backdrop to it, your whole past *before* that, is as misty as the moors in November. Didn't it bother you *then* that there were these blank spots?"

"My entire past isn't gone, just key areas, and I can only say that I didn't notice their absence then. One doesn't miss something, after all, until one begins looking for it. Possibly I'd been specifically instructed not to go delving where they had excavated. By . . ." He smiled wryly. "I've blocked the word."

"By post-hypnotic suggestion?" she suggested.

He nodded, saying no more.

"Yes. Yes, there would have had to have been something like that, if your story is to make any sense. Even so, I'm still suspicious about that evening. The focus is too sharp, and the colors are too clear. It's like a good Hollywood movie where everything is more real than reality. What I would suggest is this–that the whole thing, all that you think you remember about me, including the dinner, was fashioned right here in this Village, either on the day you arrived (for you admit to waking in the station without quite knowing how you'd got there), or else you never left the Village *at all*. The whole interlude in London was a dream, an illusion *they* manufactured. You'll notice that my theory doesn't require two sets of *theys*."

"Why stop there? An even simpler theory would be that my entire life has been a dream."

"And mine as well. Or we may both be figures in some larger dream, though that won't solve our problems, for surely the dreamer dreaming us will require us to solve his conundrums as though we were real. But whimsy aside, I'm serious in suggesting that the false memories were grafted *here*."

"To what end?" he asked.

"We'd have to know to what larger end we are their means in order to answer that. Perhaps it's enough that we should be asking ourselves questions like these. What is real? Who am I? Do I wake or dream? Then, when we're hopelessly muddled, they'll tell us the answers they've already prepared."

"All right, that takes care of my case. I'll agree that if my memory of you is false, it was falsified here. *Now*, what if it is your memories that have been remodeled?"

"In principle it would amount to the same thing. There's no problem, in my case, as to when they could have gone to work on me, since I did wake up in the hospital. However, with me they'd have had to revise a lifetime's memories; for you they need only insert a chapter entitled 'Liora' here and there. How important *was* she to you? Were you in love?"

"In and out. We see-sawed very skillfully, so that we seldom were both in at the same time, or out."

"That much sounds like me, at least. What particulars can you tell me about her? For instance, was she married or single?"

"We tried not to be inquisitive. When we were alone, we would pretend that our lives were uncomplicated. I believed you were single."

"I'm divorced, twice over. When did you meet her? What things did you do together?"

"I remember our first meeting quite well. But I should remind you that we probably have listeners. There are more bugs in this cottage than in an embassy in Washington. It must have been in order that one of us should start answering such questions that this interview was arranged. I can answer indirectly by asking you a question: have you ever been in Bergamo?"

"Bergamo...I was *through* Lombardy at different times, but eventually all those churches and palaces and piazzas, they blur. Isn't it likely that we were all in Bergamo at one time or another?"

"We?"

"People in our line of work."

"Then you admit that much at least."

It was as though he'd seen across these endless mists of speculation a single, real, hard-edged object, a bicycle with a dented fender, a kiosk papered with the morning's headlines.

"It's a trifling admission. You–or they–had to have *some* reason for abducting me. Even if my charms rivaled Helen's, I could have been raped without all this *equipment.*"

"Then there's nothing in my story that relates to the world *you* know? If you're Liora, they can't have reshaped your entire past. The easiest thing would have been for them to chop out the scenes where I appear and fill up any cracks with putty. But they can't have filled all the cracks. Life, even when it seems fragmented, is too much of a piece to allow such operations not to leave scars."

She sighed. "We have to do this, don't we? God, if I'd thought when I began my life of sin, that I'd be spending an evening like this some day, hearing the whole thing played back at the wrong speed, I'd have stayed at the University and taught courses in Pound and Eliot. Well, if we must we must, but do try and act more like the bewitched, bewildered lover you claim to be and bring me another drink, that's a mercy."

He described, for Lorna, the Liora he remembered: her flat on Chandos Place, and its furnishings; the names and characters of maids she had employed; her preferences in art and music. He recounted the day, years before, that he had accompenied her to the V & A to have a teapot identified: she'd been told it was New Hall and quite valuable.

"That *couldn't* be me," she protested. "I know nothing about porcelain and care less."

"And cathedrals? You were always driving off to the cathedral towns."

She shrugged. "I go into any great pile of masonry when it's put in my path, but I wouldn't drive ten miles out of my way for St. Peter's itself."

"You don't know Salisbury? Or Winchester? Or Wells?"

"I know Americans used to be hot for such cultural plums, but that was a *century* ago. This Liora of yours sounds like a heroine in Henry James."

"Liora couldn't read James. She said he was antiquated."

"And I've read *all* of him. Also, I gather from your account of the dinner that she fancied herself a gourmet.

While my friends have been known to say behind my back that *I* have a wooden palate. But continue with your portrait: eventually you'll have to see it doesn't represent me."

He inventoried, as best he could, clothes he'd seen Liora wearing, and Lorna contradicted each blouse, slip, and scarf on his list.

"And," she added, "the most damning evidence, as I see it, is that you say you're familiar with everything I'm wearing *now*. I'm reminded of the way ducklings learn to know their mother. There's a crucial moment just after they hatch when their brains are *printed* with the image of any large moving thing about them, and that thing, whatever it may be, becomes 'Mother.' I'm beginning to believe that there was a Liora, once, somewhere. Your description is too circumstantial to be entirely fanciful. What *they've* done is to erase the face in the portrait; then, when I arrived, they triggered the *printing* mechanism, so that my face, the physical me including the mannerisms and tricks of speech you say are hers, became your new definition of 'Liora.' They might have selected me on account of some point of resemblance, or, as I'd prefer to think, they rummaged in your past for the woman who most resembled *me*. I have enough vanity to want to be the focus of their scheming, rather than a convenient rack to hang your memories on."

"I'll admit that the evidence, as it piles up—"

"As it doesn't," she corrected.

"I'll admit it looks damning," he went on. "But who does it damn? *I* don't know."

"You really do want to find a way out for both of us, don't you? You don't *want* to think ill of me."

"Yes, I'm that big a fool. I like you too much, even—" He

turned away from her angrily, though his anger was not with her.

She caught hold of his hand. "Even as Lorna?"

The hands tightened about each other.

"So. You like me too much. And love . . . does that come into it? No, don't answer, just let me see your eyes."

Once more they stared at each other in the incandescent glare, and this time each of them supposed he saw, behind the masks, a kind of truthfulness, the real face of the other person.

"Yes," she said, lowering her eyes, "*something* registers. Not a memory, though. Only a kind of sadness. I wish, I really do, that I *could* remember you. I wish . . . if we could just *ignore* the past. No, I see we can't."

"Isn't *this* a kind of proof?" he insisted. "You don't strike me, even doubly divorced, as someone who falls headlong in love."

"A proof? Even if I let myself believe your story, Number 6, I'd have to doubt your intentions. Lovers can commit treason. Especially lovers."

Her hand had grown slack in his. He placed it on the arm of her chair.

"They can," he admitted. "I've seen it happen."

"Though even then, a kind of love survives. Judas, for instance, might have felt a terrible tenderness at the moment of that kiss."

"He might have. Though he forfeited, with the same kiss, any claim to have its sincerity believed."

"Belief! All my life I've wanted to *believe* things. Knowledge always gets in the way. I want to believe you knew me, that we were in love. I want to believe I was the princess you described, with my own–what kind of teapot was it?"

"New Hall. You found it on Portobello Road for just ten pounds."

"How clever of the person I wish I'd been. I want to have had a posh flat just off the Strand, and a number that isn't listed in the Directory. What was it, by the way? It's details like that will make me really belive in your Liora."

"COVentry-6121."

The hands tensed; fingers knotted about the slender bowed mahogany. Her face froze into a sudden mask of disinterested curiosity; terror swirled beneath the brittle surface. "You called me at that number . . . often?"

"Often, off and on."

"When was the last time you rang it?"

"When I was in London last Friday. It had been disconnected."

"But you said, before, something about a wrong number. You talked to someone at a bookshop. What did they say to you?"

"Only that I had a wrong number." The memory rested, invisible, on a high shelf: by streching, his fingertips could brush its edges.

"What bookshop? Who spoke to you?"

It tumbled off the shelf and shattered: a stain spread across the carpet. "A woman. And it wasn't a wrong number, exactly. The first three letters of the exchange were the same, but I'd given it a different name. It was you?"

"It was me. I'd completely forgotten that. I only remember how you made me go to some sort of trouble. You said you were calling from out of town."

"From here. It was the day I arrived. But—why did you pretend to be a bookclerk?"

"I *was* at Better Books. Look in the directory—that's it's number."

"But you're *not* a bookclerk!"

"A friend of mine was to give a reading there that evening, a poet. He'd gone into the basement with the manager and left me to look after the counter. The shop was empty. That's how I *happened* to answer the phone. My God, I can remember almost every word of it now! I thought it was some tedious practical joke. You made me look down the list of exchanges to make certain there wasn't a COVentry exchange somewhere in the suburbs."

"How long were you in the shop, altogether?"

"Not five minutes. That was the only call I answered. How did you pick just that moment to call?"

"It was completely spontaneous. Completely, Liora. I'd been sitting at the—"

"Damn it, don't call me Liora!"

"But this means you are Liora. It's the link we were looking for. It's the one crack they forgot to putty."

"It's nothing of the sort. My presence in the shop was just as unpremeditated. We'd been up and down Charing Cross all that afternoon, and we only stopped in to pick up posters for the reading. I didn't even return that evening. Only someone who'd followed me would have known I was there. *When you called.*"

"It's not possible. We couldn't both just *happen* to—"

"No, we couldn't. It's certain that one of us is lying. It's certain."

"But why would either of us tell such a foolish lie? Why

would I have mentioned making the call, if I'm lying? Just to be proven a liar?"

"No, I *won't* go through all this again. I refuse to. I'm very tired. I was told that you'd show me where I'm supposed to stay. Needless to say, I can't accept the offer of your *private* hospitality."

"Liora, or Lorna if you prefer—I *believe* you now. That is—"

"That is, you believe I'm sincere in my delusions. And you want to help me become my old self again. And when you've restored me to my former glory, what then, eh? How do you intend to *use* me?"

"Believe me, I—"

"Believe you? I understand that if you torture a person long enough, you can make them believe anything. We don't call it torture now, though. What is the pleasanter term they've adopted? Behavior therapy. I suggest you try that."

"I want to help you. I'll do anything I can help you. I can't be plainer than that."

"There's one thing you can do to help me, Number 6—set me free."

"I'm not your jailer, Liora. I am . . . a prisoner."

He had refused, before, to say this in just so many words. Now, the proposition seemed inarguable: he *was* a prisoner. He could not set another free when he was not free himself.

And he was not free.

"Then," she said scornfully, "if you're determined to keep up your role of 'prisoner,' help me to escape. You say you've managed one escape for yourself. Manage one for me."

"Yes, I'll do that. We can't discuss it, here, for the reason

I explained. But I have another notion, and we should be able to bring it off. With a little help."

"Not *we*, my would-be-darling-*me*. You'll help me escape, all by myself. If I left here with you, how would I ever know I'd escaped?"

"I'll go that far too. I'll help you escape by yourself."

"And, if you do, and you succeed, I might even come to believe you. Eventually."

"When, later on, I get out of here myself..."

She shook her head sadly. "A rendezvous?" As she spoke it, the word took on an almost tangible quality, as though what he'd offered her as a diamond she'd handed back to him in an envelope, a powder of paste.

"Not immediately," he assured her. "We could let a year go by."

"An entire year? And where should we celebrate the anniversary of my escape? At the terrace restaurant? In the hospital? Then we might invite the pretty white-haired doctor."

"All right, we'll make no plans. It may come about by chance."

"I don't know, after this evening, if I'll ever believe in chance again. Enough! Take me to my hotel now. I'm sure the warden is beginning to worry about me."

She rose from the chair. They stood beside each other, close enough to embrace, without embracing, yet without moving apart.

"I'll have to call one of their taxis," he said. "We aren't permitted to walk the streets after curfew. The patrols are not friendly."

But he did not go toward the telephone, nor did she seem to expect him to.

"You'll have your memories, at least," she said, in a softer voice. "I'll have nothing. Not even my own identity, if what you say is true."

"You'll have your freedom. You want it, don't you?"

"Yes." She smiled bittersweetly, touching the emerald pendant on her throat. "And at any price."

He remembered, after she had left, her words that evening at the Connaught: *If you can't trust me, you'll never be able to trust anyone.* It summed up the situation nicely.

Had she, that long ago, meant it to?

Chapter Fourteen

Number 14

"Come in, Number 6," the doctor said, snapping shut her compact, "and take off your clothes. Thank you for being so punctual."

"Thank the guards who brought me."

"You're *looking* very well," she said, handing him a hanger for his trousers.

"Shouldn't I? Was I infected with something the last time I was here?"

"So far as I know this hospital has never had a single case of staph infection, if that's what you mean. This is only a routine examination. Let me see your tongue."

He stuck out his tongue. She wrote something on the card clipped to her board.

"What did you write on the card?" he asked, once his tongue was back in his mouth.

"That it's pink. You show no *symptoms* of any kind?"

"None."

"Palpitations? Giddiness? Shortness of breath? *Tension?*"

"Not a trace."

"Your dreams?"

"Exhibit neither sex nor violence. The entire family could be allowed to see them."

She tossed back waves of white hair to plug a stethoscope in her ears for auscultation. He breathed slowly or rapidly as she required.

"I hear so much from my brother," she chattered, as though his internal processes were of interest to her only as background music, "about the lively process you've set in motion. I've never seen him work so hard at anything before. And not only my brother–everyone seems to be catching fever from it. Now breathe quickly. Yes, like that. What I couldn't understand is why *you* should have become, all of a sudden, so civic-minded. When I last saw you, at your cottage, you showed something bordering on contempt for the greatness we were thrusting on you. Now, cough."

He coughed.

"And again. Good. You can talk now." She scribbled numbers on the card.

"Can I get dressed?"

"No, there are still your reflexes to be tested. Sit up there where your feet can dangle, and tell me about your change of heart."

"It's no change of heart. I'm doing this for myself, not for the Village. Ever since college, where I did a bit of acting, I've wanted to direct this play. There was seldom opportunity and never time. Here, there is plenty of time, and your brother, by arranging all the business of permits, rehearsal space and the rest of that, has provided the opportunity. It was his idea more than mine."

"Not to hear him speak of it. I must say you've rewarded him handsomely enough: the *two* best parts in the play."

"Your brother is a born actor."

"The cast is complete now?"

"Very nearly. I had to take the Duke's part myself. No one else would audition for it."

"My brother says it's an awful role–hundreds of lines and every one pure lead. The Duke, by his account, just goes around during the whole play, dressed up like a monk, doing nice things and *saying* nice things. Whereas Angelo is a *monster* of wickedness and hypocrisy."

"Is that your interpretation or your brother's?"

"Not mine–I never interpret anything but dreams. Is it a wrong interpretation? I read Shakespeare so long ago that all the plays are muddled together, the comedies especially. I remember that everyone sings a lot and runs around disguised as someone of the opposite sex, and that in the last act they're all obliged to get married. *Measure for Measure*–isn't that the one in the Forest of Arden?"

"No, Vienna. Half the action is set in the city prison. It's the darkest of the comedies. In fact, the chief thing that makes it a comedy is that everyone *is* obliged to get married in the last act."

"In a prison! Then it's meant to be *edifying!* A kind of protest, in fact?" She tapped his kneecap with a ballpeen hammer. His foot jerked reflexively.

"There are correspondences to the world we know. In Shakespeare there always are. But I won't underline them. The play speaks for itself."

"The people in this prison, *ought* they to be there? That will be crucial, if it's to be effective propaganda. In my own experience, I've never found anyone in prison who doesn't really belong there. Sometimes, as in your case, they must go to the most extraordinary lengths to get in, but once they've made it you can see they were always meant to be prisoners. Would Shakespeare agree?"

"On anything concerned with the problem of authority, Shakespeare has two opinions. In this case, everyone in the prison has done something to deserve to be there, but—"

"Then I'm surprised you've chosen this play. The way you keep harping on this matter of *your* innocence and *our* injustice—"

"—*but* its central theme is the gross injustice of the person in charge of the prison."

"My brother?"

"Angelo, yes. There is, as well, a heroine of unimpeachable innocence, whom this Angelo abuses in the worst way."

"Don't tell me—he seduces her."

"He tries his damnedest. She has come to him, from the convent where she's a novitiate, to plead for her brother's life. Angelo has condemned him to death."

"That's the other part my brother's playing, the condemned brother?"

"Yes, Claudio and Angelo are never on the stage together until the very end of the last act, when neither of them has much to say. I thought there was a certain fitness in having the same actor play both the judge and the condemned man, particularly as Claudio's crime is the same as Angelo's."

"Claudio was . . . concupiscent?"

"That, and carelessness."

"Playwrights always take these matters so much more

seriously than the rest of us." Meditatively, she tapped his other knee with her hammer. The foot jounced. "Well, perhaps they have to, if they're to go on writing plays. Surely, the sensible thing for Claudio and his girlfriend to have done, even in Shakespeare's day, was to get married."

"Claudio offers to, the girl is more than willing, and Isabella also tries to convince Angelo of this, when she pleads her brother's case."

"And *that's* when Angelo tries to seduce her. Oh, he is wicked! The story seems to be coming back to me now. Angelo promises to spare Claudio's life on condition that Isabella surrenders her virtue to him, and when she goes to the dungeon to tell her brother about it, *he* tries to persuade her to *do* it. But does she? I remember it both ways–she does and she doesn't."

"You'll have to come and see the play."

"I suppose your new friend–or your old friend, whichever turns out to be the case–the lady with the black hair, has been handed the plum of Isabella."

"She read for the part, but she doesn't have the voice for the grand Shakespearean manner. She'll be Mariana, and even in that role she'll be straining."

"So the most important part in the play is still open?"

"It's gaping."

"Good! That's what my brother told me, and I just wanted to be sure. You can put your pants on now. That was the *real* reason I had you brought in. I have a copy in the desk drawer, and I want to audition. Now."

"Would you have time, with your professional duties–"

"I have time, in this Village, for anything, and to spare. If it came to that, I'd rather pretend to be an actress than to go on being a doctor in real life. I love theatricals, however amateur. When we were little, my brother and I did hundreds of plays together for our parents. Besides, if he's to be Claudio, it's only proper that his sister should play Isabella."

"Perhaps. But when he's Angelo . . ."

"That's no problem. Even when we had other children in our productions, Poppa insisted that if there were any scenes that threatened propriety, my brother and I had to act them, since there could not be question, between us, of anything indiscreet. Isabella doesn't end up marrying Angelo, does she? That wouldn't be a happy ending."

"No, she marries the Duke."

"Then I must have the part. I'd *love* to marry you."

"Doesn't taste forbid that a doctor propose so shortly after a medical examination?"

"What taste forbids, Number 6, appetite excuses. Seriously, although I'll admit it's hard to be serious about a thing like marriage, I like you. Even something a bit more than that. Didn't my brother *tell* you? I told him to."

"No. He must have been too embarrassed."

"Is it so impossible to credit? That little waitress is still in love with you, as you must know, despite the way you abused her confidence when you escaped. You've given *her* a part in the play, haven't you? And Number 41 is Mariana, even though you'll have to teach her how to pronounce the words. Make me Isabella, and you'll have every female in the cast in love with you. Isn't that the principle most directors go by?"

"There's still Mistress Overdone, and I don't think our ex-Mayoress has any designs on me."

"The way she flirted with you at your open house? Her husband was giddy with jealousy. Every other time I've seen Number 34, the man's been as taciturn as granite, and though she can be talkative enough, it's usually with other mathematicians about the problems of higher mathematics, trigonometry and such."

"*She's* a mathematician?"

"I'm told she's brilliant. But with you she becomes a giggling schoolgirl. You have that effect on women. You can't pretend you didn't know that, not the way you exploit it."

"How have I exploited it in your case?"

"By assuming that I'll go on keeping your secret."

"Which is?"

"That you *were* the one who set fire to the films in the church crypt. Number 2 has been worried silly trying to establish that fact."

"I'm afraid I don't follow you."

"You needn't be disingenuous with me. You knew I was auditing your dreams that day, and you understood how we were directing them. Surely you must have figured out by now *where* we were directing them."

"As a matter of fact I wasn't able to. Whether or not I did in fact set a fire where you say, Number 2 never seemed to doubt that I did."

"Number 2 doesn't doubt it, but Number 1 apparently is unconvinced. I gather that Number 2 thinks Number 1 thinks he did it."

"Is that what you think?"

She smiled, pressing the ballpeen hammer to her lips. "I don't have to think—I *know*. But, as I was beginning to fall in love with you even then, I didn't tell. You still don't believe me; why is that?"

"Because if it were a 'secret,' you would want to keep it. You wouldn't be speaking of it now, in front of the bugs."

"Oh, that! That's one of the advantages of having a trustworthy staff. My Number 28 can perform wonders with electronics. When I need privacy, I can get it. You don't think I'd declare my passion to you on television! It would destroy the reputation I've been so long building."

"You would if you were told to. In any case, as declarations of passion go, it's a rather tepid thing."

"I got your clothes off, Number 6. To have gone any further without your cooperation would have exceeded a woman's strength. If *this* was tepid, your rencontre with Number 41 was quick-frozen. Yet you seemed willing enough to credit what she said, and most of what she only implied."

"I know Liora."

"You *think* you know her."

"All right then, as you claim to be speaking to me in confidence, tell me–do I know her? Ought I to believe, if not in her story, in her candour?"

"On principle you should never believe in a woman's candour. As to whether she's who you think she is or who she says she is, anything I told you would only add to the confusion. Even assuming you would believe in *my* candour (and remember, I'm a woman with a woman's best motive for deceiving you), how can we be sure that I know the truth in this case? I'm told only as much as *they* want me to know, and that often includes a great quantity of falsehood. I could read you the list of *names* in her dossier. Or I could–"

"Just answer this one question–why did I call that bookshop? Why was *that* number in my head?"

"*I* didn't put it there. I had nothing to do with your case till you were brought back from London two weeks ago. Beyond that, it's all speculation, fog, and upset stomach. You shouldn't take these things so seriously, Number 6–what is true, what isn't true. Doubt, as I've seen it noted in your dossier, is your Achilles' heel. Choose a truth that suits you and stick with it."

"Truth, then, should be whatever is most agreeable?"

"Has it ever been anything else? In this case, haven't you given Number 41 the benefit of your doubt, and wasn't it agreeable to do so? You love her, and you're determined to believe she loves you. I love you, and I've managed to persuade myself, against every evidence, that *at root* you must love me in return, or at least that the seeds are there. After all, look how long we've been talking together, and you haven't even started putting your shoes on. That must mean something. I entertain you. God knows, I *try* to entertain you."

"Since you're part of the establishment, I can afford to let myself be entertained by you; I could never afford to trust you."

"Did I ask you to? Trust isn't a precondition of love. In fact, in most cases, the opposite is true. I'm sure I wouldn't have grown so fond of *you*, if I weren't terribly jealous of Number 41. Do you trust *her?* You trust her even less than you do me for the sound reason that with me you know where you stand I'm one of *them*, and the fact that I'm *not* one of them makes no difference, since you'll never be convinced of it. But you needn't let that stand in the way of affection. You're putting your shoes on. You no longer are entertained. Is that because I've finally convinced you that I mean what I say?"

"It means I'm hungry. Your guards didn't give me time for lunch."

"But my audition! At least let me try out for Isabella."

"You won't have to. I think you're a great actress, and you have the part. Start learning your lines. We rehearse the first two acts tonight."

"I've already learned them, Number 6." She kissed the tip of the hammer and waved it at him. "Bye-bye. I'll see you at eight."

"Now, sister, what's the comfort?" Number 7 asked, entering the examination room a moment later by a second door.

"Why, as all comforts are: most good, most good indeed." Then, since Isabella's next lines strayed from topicality: "The play goes on, and I'm to be the leading lady."

"Have you ever been anything else? Between the two of us, there's scarcely a scene in the whole play that we can't steal. And even behind the scenes . . ."

"Will everything be ready when the curtain rises? There, I mean–on the set behind the scenes?"

"I've been busy with it all day. The hardest part is accomplished. I got the remains of the sphere (Thank God for Number 2's niggardliness!) out of the storeroom and up to the roof of the theater. Your Number 28 has already knit up the major damage, but there are still fifty little rips to be mended where it was abraded by the cliff after it had burst. We won't know for certain, of course, till everyone is in the theater and we can inflate it. You won't be afraid?" he asked in a concerned and brotherly way, a Claudio to her Isabella.

"My blood is saturated with adrenalin, but I don't know

if it's fear or the excitement. I'll feel no more afraid, certainly, at the ascent than when I have to go on as Isabella:

And have you nuns no farther privileges?"

He replied, falsetto:

"Are not these large enough?"

And she, rolling up her blue eye and her brown, ethereally:

"Yes, truly. I speak not as desiring more,
But rather wishing a more strict restraint
Upon the sisterhood, the votarists of Saint Clare."

He hopped gleefully atop the examining table. *"Then, Isabel, live chaste—"*

And she tapped out the iambs on his kneecap:

"—and, brother, die:
More than our brother is our chastity."

Wresting the hammer from her, he adopted a graver tone, judicial, sober, sanctimonious, without dimples. He became Angelo. "Did the prisoner, when he was here, exhibit any signs of *suspicion*?"

"Indeed, milord. He suspects everything, except the truth."

"He suspects *me*, in that case?"

"Not of setting this up on your own behalf, but I think he's worried that you'll betray him to Number 2. After all, have you presented him with any better motive for your helping him than altruism?"

"That's the motive he expects *me* to believe. He's going to all this trouble, he explained, for *her* sake, for Mata Hari."

"But if he's saying *that*, how can you be helping him for *his* sake?"

"I said right out that I didn't believe him, that I wasn't that naive. As soon as I explained my *real* reason for wanting him out of the Village, he admitted that they were *both* escaping, but that he couldn't tell *her*, because he'd promised her he wasn't coming."

"Do you think he does intend to take her with him?"

"We'll never know, will we?"

"And what was your *real* reason?" she asked.

"I want him far away from you, jealous, possessive brother that I am."

"And so you are."

"And, when you've left him behind, I'll have accomplished that purpose too: you will be far away from him."

"And from you. Aren't you going to miss me?"

"Terribly. You know that."

"Then why *don't* you come along?"

"Me? Why, I get dizzy just climbing a ladder. I'd die of terror in that thing. It will be bad enough to think of you sailing off like another Phaeton, or Icarus, or Medea. In any case, once you're gone they'll probably have no more use for me. I'll promise never to tattle on them, and they'll send me back to London, and we'll live happily ever after. Yes?"

She gave him a sisterly kiss. "I hope so."

He patted her hand. "You can stake your blue eyes on it. Within two weeks we'll be back together. I don't suppose you'll be returning to your old flat, not right away. Shall we set a time and place?"

"For our rendezvous? Yes–somewhere sentimental."

"The Tower of London?" he suggested.

"Another prison? That's not the sort of sentiment I had in mind. Besides, it's so big, and if the weather is nice I'd rather wait outdoors. Let's make it Westminster Bridge, on the side by Big Ben. If this were a movie, we'd *have* to meet there. So that even Americans could tell it was London."

"Once a week?"

"On Saturdays."

"At one o'clock in the afternoon."

"It's a date."

Chapter Fifteen

Measure for Measure

"My beard! Is it on straight?" Number 7 asked earnestly.

"Yes, but you've forgotten this." He reached forward and removed from the young man's hand the signet that he had, as the Duke, just entrusted to Angelo. "You're Claudio now. Remember to whine."

"The theater's full? I've been up on the roof, with 28."

"All the seats are filled, except the two we had predicted: Number 1 and 2 declined their invitations. What of the balloon?"

Number 7 edged toward the wings. The brothel scene had opened, and Mistress Overdone (Number 33) was entering, swathed in an entire rummage sale of tattered indelicacies. "It's inflating," he said absently.

"The wind?"

"Is seaward." As his tongue licked nervously at the horsehair fringe pasted beneath his nose, he reviewed with abbreviated gestures the blocking of his next scene. In proportion as he neared the stage, the play's success concerned him more than the progress of the escape.

In the brothel the First Gentleman asked Mistress Overdone: *"How now! Which of your hips has the most profound sciatica?"*

And Number 33: *"Well, well; there's one yonder arrested and carried to prison was worth five thousand of you all."*

"Who's that, I pray thee?"

"Marry, sir, that's Claudio, Signior Claudio."

"Claudio to prison? Tis not so."

"Nay," she replied, fluttering scraps of lingerie at the spotlight, *"but I know tis so. I saw him arrested, saw him carried away, and, which is more, within these three days his head to be chopped off."*

Number 7, having added the whiskers and stripped to the tights that made him Claudio, smiled just such a smile as the condemned dandy, overhearing this, might have smiled, an expression at once bright and miserable, compounded of insatiable vanity and a dying, desperate faith in the power of his own boyish charm still to prevent the worst. In the first scene, as Angelo, Number 7 had had to act; to portray Claudio nothing more seemed to be needed than that he remember to be himself.

The red beacon winked its patient message of on and off, on and off, from the spire of the church, a spike of blackness thrust against the lesser blackness of the hazed night sky. Farther away, squatting on its artificial hill, the unfenestrated mass of the administration building glowed in a perpetual twilight of mercury vapor lamps. The Village streets wove serpentine patterns of light across the nether blackness of the earth, but the cottages along these streets were uniformly dark. Even in the neutralizing darkness and from this altitude, he could not regard the place as the picture postcard it tried so hard to be: it remained the same inimical caricature he'd seen on that first taxi ride through its streets.

Behind him on the gravelled roof, the blue plastic, filling with helium, bulged and popped and lurched toward its one-time sphericity under the attentive supervision of Number 28.

On the ledge a makeshift speaker crackled the pentameters of Act III, Scene 1, a prison in Vienna.

A figure emerged from behind the swelling balloon and approached him. Shimmers of dark rayon in the darkness, slither of rayon on gravel.

"I came up to see how the work was progressing," he said. "It occurred to me that you might be here too."

"It's progressing," she said, "and I am here."

"All this time? People were beginning to worry."

"Since the start of Act II. I told Isabella–the doctor–that I was feeling queasy. She said I needed air. Once I was here I couldn't tear myself away. It's a kind of torture to watch it. Growing so slowly. I can't believe it will be all round and floating in the air in time."

"If I'd paced the first two acts any slower, the audience would never have stayed in their seats. There's not one archaic pun or proofreader's error cut from the script."

"Yes, you've done wonders drawing it out. It just goes on and on and on."

Her voice trailed off into a vacancy, which was filled by Number 14's–Isabella now–thin, wavering declamation:

> *"There spake my brother: there my father's grave*
> *Did utter forth a voice. Yes, thou must die:*
> *Thou art too noble to . . ."*

"And on," he said. "At least no one can accuse me of having done this for art's sake."

"For mine then? I'm grateful. Did I say before that I was grateful?"

"No, you didn't."

"Because I didn't believe, till now, that it wasn't all an elaborate trap. I've been waiting each day for the bite of its teeth. I shouldn't let myself believe it *now*. I look at this absurd plastic beast, and try to imagine myself lifted up by it, and carried off, and it's like . . ."

The speaker: *". . . a pond as deep as hell . . ."*

"It's like the first time my mother explained to me where babies come from. I couldn't believe that such elaborate machinery was needed to produce such a simple-seeming result. Being brought here between sleeping and waking, then leaving like *this*–I shall never believe, if I do get away, that I was here at all. And you . . ." She took one of his hands between hers, lifted it, like a housewife trying to estimate whether the weight stamped on a package was to be credited: was this *really* a full pound and a half of hamburger?

"You find *me* no more probable than the rest of this?"

"If anything, Number 6, somewhat less. I've always suspected that there were dragons in the world, but to discover, after I've been chained to the dragon's rock, that there is a Perseus as well–it's too providential. I owe you–" She paused, still weighing his hands in hers, doing calculations, reluctant to name the exact sum of her debt.

Fifty feet below, Isabella, in the chaste passion of her indignation, shook the bars of her brother's cell, a sound reduced by the speaker to the merest rattling of a die.

> *"Dost thou think, Claudio,*
> *If I would yield him my virginity,*
> *Thou mightest be freed."*

Claudio, answering, had difficulty concealing the hope that surges beneath his pious protest:

> *"O heavens! it cannot be."*

And Isabella:

> *"Yes, he would give't thee, from this rank offense,*
> *So to offend him still. This night's the time*
> *That I should do what I abhor to name,*
> *Or else thou diest tomorrow.'*

"Isn't it time you returned to them?" she asked. The sudden thaw was, as suddenly, starred with frost. "If the Duke is to enter on cue."

"There's a moment yet, and I'd rather spend it here. We won't be alone again, you and I, expect for an instant on stage, for . . ."

"Forever. Isn't that what I said? And what you've agreed to? I don't remember now how that came about. What my reasons could have been. It seemed logical then. Wouldn't *you* feel, if you were to run into me again, out there, as if this prison had breathed on you? All my talk about *distrust*–you must, if you've not been trying to deceive me, feel just the same thing toward me. The same distrust. The same reluctance."

"That's true," he said.

"Yet you would be willing, despite that—

"To see you again, out there. Yes. I'd *want* to."

She turned away from him to look across the darkened Village at the gray, gleaming planes of the administration building. "Where?"

"Wherever you like."

"Westminster Bridge?"

"That's as good a place as any."

"On the side by Big Ben. I'll go there once a week. What day?"

"Saturday, or any other."

"Saturday, then, at one o'clock in the afternoon. Do you believe me when I say. I really hope you'll be there?"

"We must try to stop asking each other, Liora, how much we believe of what we say to each other. Soon enough, *that* will be put to the test. And for now—" He opened the door to the stairwell.

They listened, attentively, to Claudio, as he sank terror-stricken into a new vice.

"*Sweet sister, let me live.*
What sin you do to save a brother's life,
Nature dispenses with the deed so far
That it becomes a virtue."

"Now the god must run downstairs to tend his machine, I know. Oh! one last thing, Number 6."

He turned, silhouetted by the fluorescence streaming from the stairwell, the hooded figure of a Franciscan monk.

"What I tried to say before, what it is I owe you." Again she hesitated at the sum, and he had time to notice that her

face, in this peculiar incidence of light, with its heavy the-
atrical makeup, was not a face he would easily have recognized. Even the self-defeated smile belonged more to
Mariana than to either the Liora he remembered of the
Lorna she claimed to be.

She averted her eyes. "An apology," she said.

"Don't mention it."

He raced down the stairs, taking each flight at two
bounds, the friar's robe bundled about his waist. He paused
two beats outside the exit to let the robe fall into place and
reached the wings at Claudio's cue:

"O hear me, Isabella."

As he stepped into the light (the judgment chamber of
the second act had become, by adding indigo filters to the
overhead spots and modifying their amperage, by replac-
ing doors with grates, by scattering a bit of straw about,
the dungeon of Act III), he reminded himself that he was no
longer who he had been a moment before: he was now a
Duke who is impersonating a friar; who pretends to
encounter as though by chance a beautiful young nun in
the condemned cell of a Viennese prison; who, bending his
head, says to her in a near whisper:

"Vouchsafe a word, young sister, but one word."

Tears trembled at the corners of the brown eye and the
blue, but she allowed no pain to be audible in her cold,
conventionally reverent reply: *"What is your will?"*

(This fleeting thought: She *is* an actress!)

Then, he was inside the play again, he was the Duke
devising Machiavellian schemes to honor clandestine
virtue and expose guilts veiled by fair appearance. Till the
curtain went down on the third act he could think no

thought of his own. Mariana's cottage was being wheeled into position for the opening of ACT IV.

The lighting now (and throughout the play) bore out his contention that this was the blackest of Shakespeare's comedies. The audience would have difficulty, from more than a few rows back, to distinguish this crumb of decayed gingerbread from the dark prison walls just visible behind it.

He felt a hand in his and gave a reassuring squeeze before he realized it was the Doctor–Isabella–Number 14.

"How am I doing?" she asked.

He mustered a smile. "Innocence was never threatened so magnificently." And let go of her hand.

Another hand: on his shoulder: Number 7, wearing scraps of the elegance Claudio had preened at his entrance in Act I. He whispered into the monk's cowl: "It sprang a leak."

This was (he thought) the instant of treachery he had been waiting for all this time. His fist clenched (he did not think) around the golden tatters.

"It's fixed!" Number 7 cried aloud. "For God's sake, don't *hit* me!"

The stage manager, in the wings opposite them, made frantic hand-signals: The curtain? The curtain?

"Where is Liora?" he demanded.

"*Number 41* is on the set–waiting, like all the rest of us, for the *curtain* to go up," he answered reproachfully. "The intermission has lasted fifteen minutes. If you hold things up much longer, you'll have the entire theater *wondering.* I've never seen you like this, Number 6."

He signaled back to the stage manager. As the curtain

rose, a snare drum trembled in the pit; then, in unison, tenor recorder and horn d'amour, in their lowest registers, sounded the slow triads of Mariana's song. The simple melody swelled, ebbed, faded back into the knife-edge rolling of the drum, across which Liora's piercing, flawed soprano traced the same mournful pattern:

"Take, O take those lips away,
That so sweetly were forsworn . . ."

His hand still gripped the ragged collar, and he shook Number 7 back and forth to the rhythm of his words, the rhythm of Mariana's song: "Now tell me, again, and coherently, what *happened* up there?"

"Nothing. Really. A false alarm." He writhed and groveled, whined and smiled, never departing from the character of Claudio. "Number 28 is fixing it now. He's *finished* fixing it. Just a *little* leak. The balloon's already in the *air*."

"How long a delay will this mean?"

"And those eyes, the break of day,
Lights that do mislead the morn . . ."

"Five minutes at most, he says. But it will be ready at the curtain call, and you can't go up to the roof till then, in any case. It doesn't change a thing."

"It means that she'll panic."

"So? You needn't tell her. It's not the delay that upsets you, is it? You thought I'd sabotaged your project. Admit it."

"Damn." And, on reconsideration: "Damn!"

At the refrain, recorder and horn again joined the song, moving first in opposition to the soprano's ascending melody, then, as though she could not resist their downward impulse, uniting with it in a slow decline to silence:

"But my kisses bring again, bring again,
Seals of love, but seal'd in vain, seal'd in vain."

"That's your cue," Number 7 said.

It was. It was his cue.

"What was *that* all about?" the doctor asked her brother, as soon as the Duke had begun to deliver his lines.

"A little game, a bit of amusement."

"We shouldn't go out of our way, you know, to worry him," she said, worriedly. "*Did* it have a leak?"

"Of course not."

"Then why on earth—"

"Don't raise your voice," he said loudly. (With his sister he seemed to prefer to take the role of Angelo.) "He'll hear you."

"It will only make him more *anxious* to get up there the minute the curtain comes down—and that much harder for *me*."

"I've told you that that's already taken care of. Don't, don't, don't *fret!* Stop acting like yourself, and act like Isabella. You're *on*, in seconds. Good lord, you can't collapse *now*. This is the crucial moment of our own little play, symbolically: this is where it's arranged for you and Mariana to exchange places. Get out there, darling—and break your leg. *Now!*"

The doctor stumbled in the wings; Isabella walked gravely on to the stage, a symbolic moment that was, after all, only one among many.

Shortly afterward, it was another woman who stood with Number 7.

"Can they see us from where they are?" he asked.

"No. I tried to all through my song. You were so *loud*—you nearly ruined it."

"Does that matter? *We* won't be here to read the reviews."

She stood on tiptoes, waiting.

"You're *sure* they can't see us?" he asked teasingly.

"I wish they *could*."

He kissed her: the exchange had been completed.

"Do you love me?" he asked.

"Love *you?*" she asked incredulously. "Don't be silly–I love him."

"Then shouldn't you save your kisses, my dear Judas, for him?"

"I save a special kind for him. Do *you* love *me?*"

"Don't be silly," he said. "I love ..." He had to stop and consider.

Meanwhile, before the painted door of the canvas cottage, Isabella was explaining, to the disguised Duke, the arrangement she had made for her night in Angelo's bed, an appointment which the Duke would then have to persuade Mariana (who had been, years before, compromised and abandoned by that same villain, when her dowry had been lost at sea) to keep in her stead. By such devious means (the false friar assured her) would virtue emerge not only triumphant but unscathed.

Reluctantly, as though she still were not fully persuaded that virtue could be so oblique, she repeated Angelo's instructions:

> "He hath a garden circummur'd with brick,
> Whose western side is with a vineyard back'd;
> And to that vineyard is a planched gate,
> That makes his opening with this bigger key.

This other doth command a little door
Which from the vineyard to the garden leads.
There have I made my promise,
Upon the heavy middle of the night,
To call upon him."

Chapter Sixteen

Act V, and After

Isabella has made her accusations against Angelo, Mariana has confirmed them, and the Duke has revealed himself to have been the Friar who arranged the details of Mariana's assignation.

Only the denouement remains.

"Sir," he said to Angelo, *"by your leave."* He paused to gather fresh thunderbolts, while the guilty deputy, revealed, disgraced, curled into a heap of abasement at his feet.

> *"Hast thou or word, or wit, or impudence*
> *That yet can do thee office? If thou hast,*
> *Rely upon it till my tale be heard,*
> *And hold no longer out."*

Angelo's sternness, turning against itself, became the cringing of Claudio:

> *"O my dread lord!*
> *I should be guiltier than my guiltiness*
> *To think I can be undiscernible,*

When I perceive your Grace, like power divine,
Hath looked upon my passes. Then, good Prince,
No longer session hold upon my shame,
But let my trial be my own confession.
Immediate sentence, then, and sequent death
Is all the grace I beg."

He gestured sternly to Liora. *"Come hither, Mariana."*

Reluctantly she released the Doctor's hand to step forward a pace, two. She seemed acutely sensible of her own guilt in creating this scene, as though not justice but revenge had been her motive in helping to bring Angelo this low.

"Say," the Duke demanded of Angelo, *"wast thou ere contracted to this woman?"*

Angelo, in the fury of his penitence, had knocked his eyeglasses to the stage. Squinting, he moved toward her on his knees.

Liora–Lorna–Number 41–Mariana took a third step forward.

"I was, my lord."

"Go and take her hence, and marry her instantly.
Do you the office, Friar–which consumate,
Return him here again. Go with him, Provost."

Exeunt Number 7 and Liora, flanked by a monk and the prison warden.

He stepped down from the rude wooden platform erected on this make-believe highway that looked remarkably like a brothel, a judgment chamber and a prison.

At the Duke's first step toward Isabella these multivalent walls were to begin their slow evaporation, while the lights would mount toward an afternoon brightness. He waited for the man at the light box to pick up his cue.

In the expectant silence he could hear, off-stage, the opening and closing of a door.

At his next step the light dimmed. The small crowd of Officers, Citizens and Attendants assembled on the stage shifted uneasily.

There was no help for it: he began the brief scene in which the Duke, not done dissembling, condoles with Isabella for the death of her brother (who isn't dead). By his last line–*"Make it your comfort, so happy is your brother."*–thick night had palled the stage in the dunnest smoke of hell. A single feeble spot picked out the faces of the Duke and Isabella.

Angelo and Mariana returned (bound in wedlock), a black shimmer of velveteen, a sheen of black rayon. Contrary to his own blocking, he approached the pair of them as he pronounced the sentence (which he would, a moment later, revoke): " *'An Angelo for Claudio, death for death!'* " Angelo collapsed, throwing his arms over his head (another departure from the acting script), while Mariana backed away from him along the edge of the apron until her long gown had snagged in the extinguished footlights.

He repeated her cue: *"Away with him!"*

"O, my most gracious lord!" the blond waitress cried, with genuine terror. *"I hope you will not mock me . . . with a husband."*

The Duke's pause exceeded Mariana's in its unreasonableness. Even the most tolerant members of the audience were beginning to think this an eccentric interpretation to judge by the sudden epidemic of coughing from the orchestra and balcony.

Recalling that the balloon would not be ready to ascend before the curtain fell, he decided to continue to be the

Duke. The play was near its end, in any case. The few moments' head-start she'd won by having Number 127 stand in for her would not, probably, prove to be decisive.

When the Duke began speaking again, his delivery was more eccentric than his sudden, unaccountable silence. It was almost as hard to distinguish the words rushing past as it was to make out the faces of the actors on the darkened stage, and even when the words could be sorted out their sense could not be, for he was omitting phrases, lines, entire speeches seemingly at random. When Isabella and Mariana tried to plead in Angelo's behalf, he interrupted at their first pause for breath. He dispatched the Provost off-stage to resurrect Claudio, and a full minute before he had returned (barely in time for the end) he addressed the darkness as though it already contained Claudio (as, for all anyone in the audience could tell, it might have).

With a final admonition to Angelo to love his wife (omitting the final scene with Lucio, as he had skipped past Escalus already), he began the Duke's concluding speech. It went by, like a racing car, in a single blur of blank verse, braking only as he reached the last six lines of the play. This much, a few seconds, he was willing to sacrifice for art's sake:

> *"Dear Isabel,*
> *I have a motion much imports your good,*
> *Whereto if you'll a willing ear incline,*
> *What's mine is yours, and what is yours is mine.*
> *So, bring us to your palace, where we'll show*
> *What's yet behind, that's meet you all should know."*

By sticking out the play to its end he had lost, at most, two and a half minutes. Now, as soon as the curtain dropped . . .

Instead, in floods of light, the audience rose, as though it had often rehearsed this moment, clapping and cheering, and the cast surrounded him. Hands wrapped about his arms and legs, lifted him into the air, placed him on the shoulders of the Provost and Lucio, who carried him forward in triumph to the foot of the stage. The applause swelled. Flowers arced upward, fell to the stage and into the pit. The last row of the balcony began stamping its communal feet, and soon the entire theater had taken up the steady, stupefying rhythm.

Not till Angelo had stepped forward for his second stand-call did he notice that it was not Number 7 in Angelo's velveteen robes, but the doctor's assistant, Number 28, who had prepared the balloon for its ascent. Likewise (as 7's double role had required), it was another actor who received the applause for Claudio.

This was a possibility he had never once imagined, and what he found so astonishing now was not their collusion but his own guilelessness: never *once!*

When he had stopped trying to squirm down off their shoulders, they lowered him of their own accord. Hand in hand with the leading lady, he took several calls. She was presented with an enormous bouquet of roses, white and red together as at a funeral. He was given a plaque, with his number etched on the gilt plate beneath two masks, one that smiled and one that frowned.

The ovation went on for fifteen minutes before the curtain was allowed to come down.

Number 14 regarded the bouquet in her arms with a look of aversion. She seemed about to fling it to the floor. Then, with a more considered contempt, she let it drop.

They had been left alone on the stage. The cast and

stage hands had gone downstairs to their party, while on the other side of the curtains the audience squeezed itself out in a thick human paste through the exits into the lobby and the night streets.

"There's no point, is there, going up there?"

He shook his head. "They've gone."

"And I'm here, and you're here, like two punchlines without their jokes."

"Am I to believe, now, that you—"

"Believe whatever you care to, Number 6." She laughed, almost lightheartedly. "You know, he must regret that he's missing *this*. It's the sort of thing that would tickle him." Wearily she zipped open her costume, pulled it over her head. She was wearing, beneath the novitiate's habit, slacks and a heavy wool shirt.

"This?"

"Us, now, here. Oh, for pity's sake, can't you see—they foxed me *too*. He'd made me think it would be *my* escape, just the way he led you along the whole long way he wanted you to go. You haven't really been doing all this on *her* account, have you? You wouldn't look so chagrined, if that were so. The balloon was supposed to be for *you*, wasn't it?"

"I—" He could see the explanation stretching on to the horizon and decided that an answer would be simpler. "Yes."

"Alone?"

"I don't know. Up to the last minute I couldn't decide. Earlier tonight when I saw her on the roof, I almost let myself believe—"

"No doubt she felt sorry for you then."

"I wonder," he began (an entire chorus of alluring Possibilities waved scarves at him from that horizon). But a glance at the doctor's eyes fixed on him, measuring him like calipers, made him break off.

"You wonder," she continued for him, "whether *they* were escaping. Or if this was just another play-within-a-play. I don't think we can ever be sure. If a play, I fail to get the point, but that happens to me at most plays."

"But if it were genuine, a *real* escape, how did he arrange all *this* on his own?" His gesture indicated only the painted prison walls, but she understood what else his words encompassed: the collusion of Number 28, of the waitress, of the cast, the stage hands, even the audience, whose enthusiasm had far exceeded anything the play might have merited on its own.

"That's so," she said. "He couldn't have done all that."

From the wings Number 98, the Stationer's clerk, approached them, still in the costume of Elbow, the foolish constable. "Number 6?" he called out hesitantly. "There was a . . ." He held it out at arm's length to show that there actually *was*. "One of the guards brought this . . . this, uh . . . I told him you were probably still . . . And I was right!"

"It will be from *him*, I expect," the doctor said. "A Parthian shot."

Number 98 handed him the sealed envelope, then turned to the doctor. "And there's this for you, Number 14." A second envelope."

Elbow waited between them, meekly curious. "A note of congratulations? I think everyone thinks that we've had a . . . tremendous . . . Although the ending . . . I can't imagine how the man at the light box could have . . . But even so, it was . . . I mean, the *audience* . . . Don't you think so?"

His eyes darted back and forth between Number 6 and Number 14, Number 14 and Number 6. His smile withered.

"I suppose," he said, repeating the lesson life had taught him in so many forms, "that you'd like to be alone now." Neither would contradict this, and he returned to the party below, shaking his head and marveling once again at the coolness of the truly great even in the very furnace of success.

She finished reading her letter first.

"It's what I expected. He jeers sincere apologies. Passion, he must confess, overwhelmed him. Is yours the same? Or did *she* write to you?"

"I don't know. Here, read it." He handed her the first page, while he continued with the second. The letter read:

My dear Number 6,

There is very little I can offer in extenuation of my conduct. That I have systematically deceived you, all the while protesting my friendship and good intentions, I cannot deny. Yet I would still protest that that friendship is real, that my intentions remain good, and that my actions were dictated by an impersonal Necessity. Isn't it true that I've taken from you no more than you would have taken from me? That is to say, the means of escape.

In my position, under a surveillance stricter than any you have known, there was no way *I* could escape unless I seemed to be playing one of the standard variations on our theme of cat-and-mouse. Do you know de L'Isle-Adam's *The Torture of Hope?* Its premise is that nothing is so conducive to despair as to allow an escape to succeed up to the very moment the prisoner breathes his first mouthful of freedom-then to spring the trap-door under his feet. That was the principle behind your "escape" to London, and it was the *stated* principle, in my official reports, behind tonight's affair, though of course in *this* case I would hesitate to trace each sub-plot to its ultimate literary source. In any case, while it must be admitted that our lives imitate art, I like to think that sometimes we may invent some little twist all our own before the novelists think of it. If not this time, perhaps the next. (My *credo*.)

You may recall having debated with me, some time ago, concerning the relative advantages enjoyed by the prisoner and his jailer. I was obliged then to present the case for the prosecution. Now, though my opinions haven't changed, my *position* has, and I am forced to concede (in my own defense) that, yes indeed, the jailer *is* less free than the prisoner, that the warden's office is also a cell of maximum security. The very fact that I must *escape* proves that I have been, like you, a prisoner-without even your solace of being able to blame someone else. (Though I have always been able to find *excuses*.) Ah, this is all philosophy, and I know how we both recoil from *that!*

Some facts, then, and a bit of explanation:

All that stuff above (the philosophy) would never have occurred to me-would never, at least, have *affected* me-without your adventure in the archives. *I* know you set that fire, *you* know you set that fire, but Number 1, whose imagination at rare moments can equal yours or mine, was not to be persuaded it was as simple as all that. There were films concerning myself destroyed then that had been used to secure my ... (Would "allegiance" be the right word?) ... to this Village (and *that* is not the right word either). Though I pointed out to Number 1 that my "allegiance" had since been secured with links of guilt (which is, I'm afraid, exactly the right word) far stronger than the trifling scandals documented in those films, Number 1 remained suspicious. After all, when the mood hits him, whom does he have to be suspicious of, except for me? Lesser suspicious can be delegated.

I could measure day by day the growing pressure, the spread of insubordination, and the steady fraying of the cord that held the sword above my head. Had I not succeeded at *this* escape, I would have had to take the advice you offered, as the Duke, and "be absolute for death." That much of an absolutist I am not.

Goodbye then. Let me express the sincere hope that we may meet again. Perhaps by then the wheel of Fortune will have turned 180 degrees, and you may enjoy (would you?) the sensation of playing Warden to my Prisoner.

Best regards,
Number 2

P.S. Concerning the technology of deception (I hope you take an interest in these details, retrospectively): My persona as a cracker-barrel philosopher was all done with electrons and a 1901 anthology called *Heart Throbs*. A character actor was hired and photographed through the entire gamut of what his face could do. This repertoire was coded into a computer. Whenever "Number 2" appeared on television, there was always a live camera on me. My expressions were translated, by the computer, into his, just as my voice was changed to his by the same method. One of my few regrets in leaving the Village is that I can't take the old duffer along. I'd become quite fond of him. Hadn't you?

P.P.S. A last word of good counsel from *Heart Throbs'* endless store:

> Should you feel inclined to censure
> Faults you may in others view,
> Ask your own heart ere you venture,
> If that has not failings, too.
>
> Do not form opinions blindly;
> Hastiness to trouble tends;
> Those of whom we thought unkindly
> Oft become our warmest friends.

"Then it was an escape, after all," she said, handing the letter back to him. "My brother couldn't have arranged a conspiracy on as large a scale as this evening's, but Number 2 could have accomplished it with three or four memoes. If irony is any comfort to you, there's this: it was the two of us, together, who put him on the skids. The fire *you* set; the betraying detail in your dream, which *I* kept back."

"You're certain it was your brother who wrote this letter?"

"Of course. You don't think . . ."

"That it was from her? Is there any evidence, in the letter, to prove it couldn't be? There isn't."

"Look more closely. There must a lapse, somewhere-some way of standing a sentence on its head, a pet word, something that's characteristic of only one of them."

"Give Number 2, whoever he is, credit for subtlety. Anything we might point to as 'characteristic' could have been planted in the letter just for us to point to. The only certain proof would be if one of us had carried on a dialogue with Number 2 while either your brother or Liora was present in the same room. I haven't. Have you?"

"No. But doesn't that make my brother the likelier suspect, in view of all the times I've been with him and all the times that Number 2 has intruded on me, at my cottage, in the lab, on the street? The coincidence seems mountainous.

"On the other hand, isn't this the best explanation of the paradoxes and impossibilities in *her* story?"

"Perhaps–but say what you will, until it's *proven* one way or the other, I'll be convinced it was him. It all seems, in hindsight, so in keeping with his *character*."

"And I'll remain convinced it was her. I imagine all of this has been devised with some care just so each of us would reach the conclusions we have."

She smiled wistfully, as though remembering a pleasant weekend spent, some years before, on a country estate subsequently destroyed in the blitz. "He *would* have enjoyed this so much.

"Or," she added politely, "*she* would have."

The last performers entered on to the stage, a six-man squad of night patrolmen. After a flourish of jackboots, the leader of the chorus (or squad) stepped forward and saluted the couple at center stage. He seemed to be waiting for orders to carry off the dead bodies. Would he believe that this had only been a comedy?

"Yes?" the doctor said.

"You are Number 14?" the squad leader asked.

"Apparently. As of this moment."

"We have orders to arrest Number 2."

"I'm afraid you've arrived well past the nick of time. Number 2 escaped, with a friend, in a helium balloon, some minutes ago."

The squad leader consulted with the members of his squad. After stomping them back to attention, he again addressed the doctor: "There appears to be a misunderstanding here, Number 14. We have orders to arrest the man standing beside you." He pointed to Number 6, standing beside her.

"You very well may have orders to arrest him, but *this* man is Number 6."

The squad leader smiled with tolerant amusement at Woman's ability to misunderstand whatever she needs to. "As of *this* moment, ma'am, that man is Number 2."

She turned to him, wavering between hilarity and bewilderment. "Have *you* been . . . All this time? No. No, not you."

She turned back to the squad leader. "May I ask what your orders are, once Number . . . 2 has been *arrested?*"

"He's to be locked up, pending further orders."

"From Number 1?"

"Our instructions, Number 14, are that we'll receive orders from you."

They looked at each other and, with better timing than in any earlier scene in the play, began to laugh. They grew helpless with laughter. Each time either of them tried to talk, nothing came out but a few sputtered syllables and then more, and more helpless, laughter.

"Pardon me, Number 14," the squad leader interposed. "Pardon me! Please, if you will, ma'am, *pardon* me!"

"Yes?" Still stifling giggles.

"We'd like to be told what we're to do with the prisoner. Where shall we take him?"

"Why–to prison, of course."

"Yes, Number 14. But–" He hunched his shoulders, as though to say: But there are so *many* prisons.

"Is there any particular prison you'd prefer, Number 6? Number 2, rather."

"One's as bad as another, it seems to me."

"Very well then–you will keep the prisoner confined to this prison until I've issued further orders."

The guard looked about suspiciously. At last, despite the pain of having to show his naïveté before a superior, he had to ask outright: "Which prison is . . . this?"

She pointed to the painted canvas. "A prison in Vienna," she explained. "See that he doesn't escape."

PART IV

COUNTDOWN

"In the dream of the man who was dreaming, the dreamed man awoke."

Jorge Luis Borges, *The Circular Ruins*

Chapter Seventeen

The Conversion

"I trust," Number 14 said, "that you can hear me, though if you can't, it's of no importance. What I say is addressed to Number 6, a person who will soon no longer exist, and who, if he can hear me, probably wishes that he could not. So I don't know why I bother saying this. Another apology? You've heard too many already, from all of us. 'I am doing,' we each say, 'what Necessity requires.' It has always seemed to me that that is rather worse than crimes committed out of a pure zest for evil. No, I'll offer no excuses.

"An explanation, that's all it is. When the worst happens, I've always thought it would be a small comfort to be informed of its exact dimensions. It's that, my faith in mere *measurements*, more than any special competence or knowledge, that makes me a scientist. Perhaps it's a faith you wouldn't share, and if this were *my* earthquake, I don't know whether I would be that interested in the seismograph readings. Perhaps in the labyrinth of my motives

what I am offering in the name of charity–this explanation–is only a new twist of the old thumbscrew. Perhaps,
perhaps, perhaps–the word multiplies itself as wantonly as
an amoeba. I won't say it again.

"When I outlined this project, it was then an abstracter
kind of crime. The prospectus was completed before I knew
that *you* existed, months before you were brought back to
the Village. I did wonder, later on, whether their decision to
retrieve you had been determined by the parameters I'd
drawn up for selecting an optimum subject. (Subject!
there's a lovely euphemism. We psychologists have
invented a richer treasure of cant than all the gentlewomen
of the 19th Century together.) If that *was* their purpose,
then they took long enough getting around to it. Perhaps–oh, I've said it!–perhaps Number 2 *was* your friend,
insofar as it must have been he (or she) who kept you from
this day for . . . how long? Over two months. Surely it's significant that the order to set to work should be issued
immediately Number 2 had escaped, departed, whatever.

"I keep saying 'they.' What I mean, of course, is Number
1. Number 1 has never been able to find a lieutenant
exactly to his taste. Either they have been enterprising and
imaginative in performing their duties, in which case they
have invariably shown an imperfect loyalty, a tendency to
place their individual interests above the interests of the
Village and of Number 1. (An orthodox faith would not
distinguish between the two.) *Or* he would be a man of
unquestionable loyalty who proved, at a moment of crisis,
to be a nincompoop. Once, Number 1 discovered a subordi-
nate who combined both failings–he was a disloyal nincompoop–but he's never found someone who was at once
fanatically loyal and a brilliant administrator. Few dictators

ever have had that good luck, with the possible exception of those four paragons of the Golden Age of Authority, the '30's and '40's.

"For a dictator nothing is impossible: that is the first tenet of orthodoxy. Number 1 decided that since he could not find an ideal 2, he would have one made to order. I was brought here expressly to design a model of this superveep and to work out a method by which that model could be converted from graphs and equations into flesh and blood. Since science hasn't yet advanced to the stage where it can create a true homunculus from raw scraps of DNA, it was clear that something like a metamorphosis was called for. It was also clear that it would be more feasible to graft loyalty to an already existing imagination than the other way round.

"Which is not all as easy as you may think. Though it would take at most 48 hours to transform you, or someone of your sort, into a perfectly loyal minion, such a transformation would virtually destroy those qualities that would make your loyalty worth having: initiative, creativity, and all those other vague words that are lumped under the heading of (that vaguest word of all) Spirit. The usual techniques of brainwashing affect these virtues the way ordinary laundering affects the more perishable kinds of clothing: at worst they are demolished, like laces, and at best they shrink, like argyle socks. The merit of *my* program is that those useful qualities will be preserved, while your loyalty is shifted, ever so gradually, from its present locus to where Number 1 would like to see it, revolving in a worshipful orbit about the sun of that exalted idea: One, Oneness, Number 1. Since your present loyalty is centered not on any particular nation, institution, or surrogate

father, but about a pantheon of *ideas*–Truth, Justice, Freedom, and the rest of the Platonic tribe–its transfer to this
new orbit will be relatively easy, for the idea of One is no
less abstract, vague and exalted than, for instance, the idea
of Freedom.

"In fact, even as I talk to you now, even as you listen,
the process has begun. Like Ishtar disrobing on her
progress through the seven gates, you, in the amniotic void
of that tank, have surrendered your senses, one by one, till
now it is only the sound of my voice that ties you to reality. When my voice ceases you will exist in an elemental
state. You have read, I'm sure, about these experiments,
and you know how people, under sensory deprivation,
become malleable as refined gold. The mind cannot tolerate a vacuum, and when the senses no longer are pumping
data in, it begins to fill up from the springs of its own
unconscious. Fantasy takes over, but not the fantasy of
dreaming, for there is no distinction now between dreaming and waking. It is the conscious mind that dreams, the
ego. And it is, at these moments, intensely suggestible.

"A picture is worth a thousand words, so let me illus-
trate my lecture with a slide or two. We need not bother,
today, with lasers and such as that. Your own imagination,
starving for images, will do our work for us.

"What shall it be? Since this is not yet the metamorphosis proper, let's choose something pretty. A marble egg.
There was a marble egg on the desk in the study of your
London flat. It was rose-colored. It rested in an egg-cup of
white china. You can see it now, that marble egg, the
swirling veins of gray, the mottled rose that shifts, as you
turn it in your hand, to pink, to a deeper rose, with here
and there an arabesque of milky white. That egg has sat on

your desk for years, growing steadily more invisible as it grew more customary, but now you see it, don't you, more clearly than you've ever seen it before? It is more *real* now than it has ever been, even though you *know*, because I'm telling you, that it is only an *imaginary* egg of unreal marble that rests in an entirely subjective egg-cup. When we set to work in earnest, I will no longer be able to remind you of that paradox.

"Now, to demonstrate the final, and crucial, mechanism. Hold the marble egg up to the light. Its loveliness increases. A little higher, and the light will be ideal.

"You did, didn't you? You held it up, because that is something you would have done without compunction back here, in the real world. The action did not contradict any principle or taste. But now, observe: Put the egg in your mouth. Do as I say, Number 2, *put it in your mouth.*

"Did you do that? Unless you have a peculiar taste for sucking marble, you did not. Such an action lies outside your character, the range of what you allow yourself to *be.* You'd be amazed at how easily that range can be moved back and forth.

"We humans are, at root, Number 2, very simple creatures. Like the computers we've fashioned in our image, we operate on a binary code of pleasure and pain, a switch marked ON and another marked OFF. Finally, everything can be reduced to one or the other, everything we've learned, everything we loathe or love, everything that forms our image of what and who we are.

"At this moment, Number 2, we have control of those switches. There are two wires fixed to your scalp, one for pain, unimaginable pain, and one for pleasure, unspeakable pleasure.

"Observe, now, what these switches do. Again I will insist that you put the marble egg in your mouth. Again you refuse. Again I insist—*put the egg in your mouth*. I do more than insist, I threaten.

"Put the egg in your mouth!

"You have not, and so I touch, gently, the switch of pain.

"I release it, and suggest, only *suggest* that you would *like* to put the marble egg in your mouth. It is, after all, in keeping with your character to do so.

"Can you feel it there now, the larger end lodged in the soft flesh beneath the tongue, the smaller end touching the roof of your mouth, a small cold ovoid of marble, in your mouth? You do feel it there, and now I touch, briefly, this switch for pleasure.

"And, oh the bliss! You realize that it is *good* to have that marble egg just where it is, in your mouth. Can you feel the goodness of it there? Can you? And I touch, again, the switch.

"If I should touch it once or twice more, you would never again be able to look at, or even imagine, a marble egg without a maniacal craving to place it in your mouth.

"That is how the human machine works. What it can be made to do depends on where we decide to drive it. The bulk of my work has consisted in drawing up that road-map. The transformation from 6 to 2 will be so imperceptible that you will never, I think, be able to detect a single bend in the road, but by the time you have arrived at your final destination, at complete Twoness, you would not be able to recognize yourself in what you have become, anymore than that new self, that perfect figure 2, will be able to see himself in you, the 'you' who hears this.

"And it will be a terrible loss, I think. Because I did love you. I loved the person that you are and that you will so soon cease to be. I doubt very much that I could love the person you're going to become. For though I know that you don't love me now, you *might* some day, and this other person we are forming from your clay will not be able to love anything but One, the idea of One's Oneness. You, who listen to me and whom I love, will have been lost to me, and to yourself.

"Goodbye, Number 6. Forgive me for my part in this. If I'd refused to play it out to the end, they would have sent an understudy on in my place. Like every other traitor, I am a coward and a pragmatist. If you were able to understand what it means to be like this, you wouldn't be here now, and I would never have loved you.

"The light is blinking above the monitor. Number 1 is impatient with my speech-making, and no doubt you are, too. We will have to begin in earnest. You can, while there is still a moment, remove the marble egg from your mouth."

Chapter Eighteen
The Marble Egg

He looked at the imaginary marble egg. It was rose-colored and streaked with grays and whites. His own fingers had lent it the warmth of their flesh.

Never once had he put the marble egg in his mouth, nor, though he had steeled himself against both, had he felt the least tingle of pleasure, the slightest twinge of pain.

He understood what she had done for him, and she had explained, in great detail, what he would now have to do for himself.

It was autumn, a brisk, tangy, delightful autumn day, and he was strolling through the park. He nodded in a cordial, absent-minded way to Number 189, the former sweeper at the railway station, who was working now for the Department of Parks. He had promoted him just last week to his new position. Number 189 acknowledged this gesture with shy, solemn respect, then returned to his work weeding hawkbit from the ordered files of the chrysanthemums.

He stopped beside the bench where the old woman was bent over her embroidery hoop. "Good *afternoon*, Granny."

She heard him the very first time and looked up with twinkles from her eyes and from the wire-frame spectacles. "Why, good afternoon, Number 2!"

"Hard at *work*, I see."

"Work? Oh yes, there's never a free moment for *me*!" With a little chuckle at her own little joke, she held the hoop up so that he might admire her handiwork.

"That's very *handsome*," he said, stooping to study the meticulously stitched orchids. "And very true to life."

"Thank you! I do love roses so–don't you?"

"Roses, well . . . yes. Do you ever embroider . . . other kinds of flowers?"

"No, just roses, Number 2. Roses have always been my favorite flower, since I was just a little snip of a thing. Red roses and white roses. I can never decide which I like better."

"It's very expert work that you do, Granny. This stitch here, for example." He pointed to one of the writhing tendrils.

"That's a scroll stitch," she confided in a low voice. "And this"–touching the dark mauve of the corolla with the tip of the needle–"is a dorando stitch."

"A dorando stitch, well, well, well." In a tone that implied that this piece of information had appreciably expanded his intellectual horizon. Patting the veined, knobby hand that held the hoop, he doled out some further sugar lumps of approbation, until all the wrinkles of her face had been brought into play by a grin of proud, senile accomplishment.

It was *clammy*, he thought, leaving her. He rubbed his

fingertips against the palm of his hand, as though that brief touch had drawn away all the warmth of his own flesh.

At the terrace restaurant he chose a seat at the table where Number 83, the male model, was playing dominoes with Number 29, the man with the goitres.

"How's it going, men?" he asked cordially.

"Great!" said the male model, with a smile that would have made anyone ready to buy the same toothpaste. "Just great, Number 2!"

"Pretty well," the goitres grumbled.

He shot one of his own smiles back at Number 83, not so broad but more confidential. "It's not hard to tell which of you is winning."

Even Number 29 had to laugh at that.

He watched their game for ten minutes, offering comments on the weather, kibbitzing when it was the goitres' turn, analyzing Number 83's performance, last Wednesday afternoon, at the big soccer match.

The waitress who brought his coffee was the red-faced woman who'd been working at the cafe by the railway station the day he'd arrived.

"Where is Number 127?" he asked with some concern.

"Oh, her!" the waitress said, with an ant's scorn for the grasshoppers of this world. "She's *sick* again."

"Has she been sick often?"

"For the last three days. It's the *flu*, she says." As she pronounced the word, "flu" became a synonym for malingering.

"Give her my regards, would you, the next time she calls in? Tell her how much we all look forward to her recovery."

The waitress sighed her consent and returned to a sink

of dirty pots, feeling somehow enriched. "It's amazing," she told herself, as she rolled up her sleeves, "how you can *always* tell a gentlemen." There was an element of sadness in this thought, for she knew that in the ordinary scheme of things such gentlemen were not for the likes of her, but even so, as long as she could bring him his cup of coffee in the afternoon, as long as there was one smile that he smiled just for her, there was some comfort to be had, there was a *point* in scrubbing all these pots.

The game of dominoes ended, and Numbers 83 and 29 rose from the table.

"Four o'clock already!" he said.

He stood to shake their hands, a handshake that made each of them realize his own special importance to the Village and to Number 2, and to what they represented. With a bemused smile, like a proud father seeing his sons set off to their work in the mines, he watched them go toward the church.

He took a deep breath of the salt air, swinging his arms up and out to stretch his tensed pectorals. His fourth set, and already he'd built up a good sweat. He took a straddle-legged position on the shingle for his next exercise. Despite all his new responsibilities, he always found the time for his morning workout and a mile's run along the beach.

At the eastern end of the crescent of shingle, near the cliff he'd scaled on that other morning (how long ago!) he saw a figure emerge out of the rocks of the cliff. A woman dressed for swimming. It was proscribed to swim at that end of the beach, where the currents were dangerous, and it was uncommon to see anyone swimming at all this late in the year or this early in the morning.

"Hallo!" he called to her.

Instead of replying by word or gesture, she ran into the dark, cliff-shadowed water.

He pressed the alarm signal on his wrist-band.

"Wait." Sprinting across the wet, shifting pebbles. "Wait a moment! Stop!"

The woman, out to thigh-depth, veered right, toward where the cliff thrust out from the shore to meet the ocean head-on. At the moment he entered the water himself, the undertow pulled her down, dragging her–and several tons of crushed stone–toward the whitecaps. He caught a glimpse of blond hair (and it was, as he had thought, the waitress, Number 127, who had been calling in ill with "flu") ten feet farther out, which vanished behind the curl of a breaking wave. He sighted her again, past the line of the surf, swimming toward the deadly roiling beauty of the cliff. He struck out in pursuit, breasting the line of the surf, gaining quickly at first, until, nearer the cliff, the varying currents mocked both their efforts, flinging them toward each other, and tearing them apart.

He caught hold of an arm. She jerked free of his grip with a convulsive strength. Screamed: "Go–" Gagged by the salt water.

A handful, then, of the blond hair. Towing her by this rope, he swam seaward against the current drawing them toward the cliff. Twisting around, she wrapped her arms about his kicking legs. They sank, interlocked, beneath the frothing surface into the stronger and stranger eddies below. Her arms were a vice of rigid, hysterical strength.

His first blow was not forceful enough. With the second she went limp.

He towed her unbuoyant body upward and surfaced,

gasping. By luck the nether currents had carried them farther from the face of the cliff, and he could swim back
toward the shore, even disadvantaged by the dead weight
of her body, without being drawn back into the area of
danger.

The patrol was inflating a life raft as he pulled her up
on to the beach. He lay on his stomach; while the gentler
water of the shore played about his ankles, he watched a
medical aide administer artificial respiration to Number
127. The guards waited respectfully until he had recovered
his breath.

"Is she all right?" he asked.

"She will be," the aide assured him, drawing his lips
away from hers to speak.

"Send out all the launches," he said, to the leader of the
patrol.

"That's been done sir." He nodded distastefully at the
woman. A mixture of vomit and brine spilled from her
unconscious lips. "Was she swimming out to meet someone?"

"Possibly. Any boat that attempted to enter the bay
would be dealt with in the usual way. What I suspect is that
the crew of one of our own patrol boats has been—"

He was interrupted by the scream of the medical aide.
He had leaped back from his patient, scrabbling across the
loose stones. Blood streamed from the deep cut in his
lower lip.

The waitress was struggling up to her elbows. Threads
of vomit still clung to the corners of her mouth and trembled as she spoke: "You needn't . . . bother . . . Number 2. I
wasn't . . . swimming out . . . to meet . . . anyone."

"What were you doing, Number 127?"

But she did not have to answer him, for their eyes had already completed the conversation. Hers had said: *Suicide*-and his replied that he had known. Hers said: *If I had the strength, I'd try and kill you again*-his told her that she'd had her chance, and failed.

"You *pig!*" she said aloud, though her eyes had said this too, and with even more force. She tried to smooth back the bedraggled hair, but the hand was smeared with her vomit. She began to cry.

"Number 2?" the medical aide asked.

"Bring her to the hospital. Number 14 will look after her now. It's all in a day's work." He turned away.

"Number 6!" she screamed, forgetting in her pain that he was no longer Number 6. "You were the *only* one, and you–" She choked as more brine welled up into her throat. By the time she had emptied herself on the wet rocks, she had realized the hopelessness of what she had been about to say.

"Sir, you don't have to walk back to the Village. Take our jeep."

"Thank you, Number 263, but I haven't had my morning run yet. Be careful with that woman. She'll probably attempt some kind of violence."

He began to trot westward, following the long shadow that glided ahead of him across the glistening pebbles, the lumps of tar, the strands of kelp, the quaking, clustered foam.

Behind him he heard her final, and definitive, curse, then her screams as she struggled with the guards.

He ran on, concentrating on his breathing. It was shallow, even, relaxed.

Entering his cottage, he found yesterday's domino-players, Numbers 83 and 29, sprawled in the Chippendale chairs, half-asleep. Automatically his hand switched on the Muzak control, and the room filled with the waltzing ghosts of a thousand animated cartoons. The goitres snorted himself to alertness, and the male model stretched himself, cat-like, and produced a very sleepy smile that would never have sold anything.

"An unexpected pleasure, gentlemen," he said.

In unison: "Good morning, Number 2."

"Tea? Coffee?"

"We've had our breakfast, thank you," said Number 29.

"You'll excuse me if I go into my bedroom to change out of these wet clothes. I won't be a minute. Here—I'll leave the door open, and you can tell me what it is that brings you to me at this unusual hour. There's no serious trouble, I hope . . . ?"

"No sir."

"Did you hear about my little adventure at the beach this morning?"

The two men exchanged a look. The younger answered. "Yes, we did, Number 2."

"Quite a stroke of luck that I was on the spot. I think the poor girl thought she was going to *swim* away!" From the bedroom, a hearty laugh. Then, as though contritely: "Of course, it's not a laughing matter. Even if it turns out that no one else was involved, an incident like this should be a lesson to all of us. If she'd gone into the water just a few minutes later, who would have seen her? Who would have brought her back? No one! Do you realize what that would have meant?"

"That she would have drowned," Number 83 said, affecting to yawn.

"Does that seem such a light matter to you?" he asked sharply, entering the living room in his everyday costume of slacks, turtleneck and jacket. "Gentlemen, an attempted suicide is a graver threat to this Village than an attempted escape. A fugitive can be brought back; a corpse cannot be."

He took a seat beside the Riesener secretaire and studied the faces of his two visitors as they chewed on this concept.

"Number 2 is right," the goitres announced, having swallowed the concept, digested it, and transported it by blood corpuscles to his brain, where it was shelved in the bulging files of Orthodox Views. In the next month he would often take the opportunity to retrieve it from the files and read it to his fellow numerals in the service of the Village-the very words addressed to *him* by Number 2.

"But how can suicide be prevented?" Number 83 asked. He did not seem to have the same digestive capacity as the goitres.

"A good question, Number 83."

Number 29 began chewing on this good question. It was going to be a full morning.

"The answer is to be found in almost every aspect of our lives here in the Village. Tell me, Number 83, are *you* happy with your life here? Does it seem *big* enough? Is it active, exciting, stimulating? Is your work as agreeable as your leisure hours?"

"Oh, *yes* sir! There's nothing that—" He raised his empty hands as a sign of his plenteous fulfillment.

"Nothing!" the goitres echoed emphatically.

"Nothing that either of you could wish for in addition to what you already have been given," he summed up for them. "In short, the Village is a kind of utopia for you, and most of us here would have to say the same thing. There is comfort and affluence. Our work is scaled to our individual capacities, and our leisure is filled to bursting with meaningful and self-improving activities. But that represents only the material aspect of the Village. There is also a spiritual aspect, which can be summed up in a single word–Oneness. The idea of Oneness should inform our every action throughout the day. It should . . . But I'm getting carried away. I know that both of you, in your own ways, treasure that idea in your inmost hearts. It's just this–the idea of Oneness–that makes our life so very much worth living that for people like *us* the notion of escape, much less of suicide, is literally unthinkable."

After a reverent silence, the goitres asked, "But in that case, Number 2, I don't understand! Why would anyone . . . ?"

"Unfortunately, Number 29, there are a *few* people in this Village–and I must confess, to my sorrow, that I used to be the worst of them–a few people who will not accept that idea, or rather–who haven't been able to *understand* it. Often the more intelligent they are, the more difficult it seems to be for them to grasp the notion of Oneness. In that respect a man like Number 189, though he may be a little slower than we are, is one of the happiest, and most *loyal*, citizens of our Village Faith is not a problem for Number 189. Of course, with the right education, faith would not be a problem for any of us. Disloyalty is only a form of *ignorance*. Always bear that in mind, gentlemen."

Loyally, the goitres filed this in the less crowded file reserved for the Eternal Truths, while Number 83 assumed his gravest expression, suitable for advertising the Great Books or an encyclopedia.

Confident that they would be occupied by these lofty

thoughts for a few minutes, he turned his chair around to face the papers spread out on the secretaire.

He froze, without knowing why, as though he'd glimpsed, with his peripheral vision, a glint of the blade above his head. His conscious mind sought for what his unconscious had already sensed.

It stood in the far left-hand corner of his desk, behind the report from the Employment Advisory Board: a marble egg, rose-colored, in a white egg-cup. A film of dust obscured the mottled grain.

My God! he thought. *How long has it been there?*

Then he recalled that last night, when he'd been working on his security recommendations, he had placed a cup of tea on the same spot, that he had left the cup and saucer there when he had gone to bed.

He spread open the folder of cost and maintenance figures of the Guardians. Reaching across the desk with apparent casualness, as an addicted smoker might reach for the cigarette he has left burning in an ashtray, he took the egg from the eggcup. He weighed it a moment in the palm of his hand, then, without seeming to notice what he did, he placed the dusty marble egg in his mouth.

Number 83 rose to his feet. "Number 2!" he said.

"Mmm?" Turning to confront him with a look of mild annoyance.

The goitres also rose, realizing from Number 83's meaningful glance toward the empty egg-cup, that the purpose of their visit had been accomplished while he'd been napping among the Eternal Truths.

Apologetically he let the egg slide out into his cupped hand. "Yes, Number 83, what is it?"

"We have instructions to accompany you to the administration building. Number 1 wishes to speak to you."

"Number 1!" he said, with an expression of transported delight that would have convinced the assembled saints in heaven that this was the real article, a bonafide Beatific Vision. "My God, why did you take all this time to *tell* me?"

"We were following our orders," the goitres explained primly. Of all the Scriptures in all his files, he liked this one the very best.

"Number 1," he repeated reverently.

And thought: *It's about time!*

Chapter Nineteen

The White Room

"Come in, Number 2," another speaker said, as he waited before another door.

The last door unlocked itself and purred upward in its steel frame, like the blade of a guillotine lifted for its next piece of work. He stepped into the white room.

Into a dazzling void, as though the lips of Reality had parted to show one last tremendous grin.

In a white alcove of this white room sat Number 1. She tilted her head sideways (a strand of white hair fell across white skin) and asked, with conscious coyness: "Are you surprised?"

"You're Number 1? *You?*"

She pursed her lips, nodded once. "You never guessed?"

"Never once. Though I always had the feeling that there was something . . . a-bit-too-much about you. But I've felt that way about everyone here."

"Come," she said. "Share this window-seat with me. We'll be friends now, you and me. As we always *should* have been."

Slowly, across the white floor, darkened not even by his own shadows, he walked toward her. He no longer kept up a pretense of holy awe, but neither did he feel inclined to rush through these concluding lines as he had done when he'd played the Duke. He had expected to feel rage at this moment, for surely rage had been mounting in him these many weeks.

Instead, he felt . . . what? Not curiosity: though he might still ask many questions, he knew better than to trust any answers, especially now that he'd made his way to the very source of all these lies. Not caution: caution had seen him as far as it could, and now, having forced the stakes to the limit, he was willing to risk everything on a single hand.

Did he suspect that this was only the penultimate imposture, not the center of labyrinth but only its antechamber? The thought had passed his mind, but to have reached even so far as the antechamber was a good second-best when he had seen no more than an outer courtyard up to now.

Was the explanation for his reticence as simple as this–that he'd been schooled, from his earliest years, to show Respect for the Aged, to whisper and to walk with a softer step in the presence of antique flesh?

Possibly. These tokens that we pay to the very old are the same that we accord to the dying. Beyond a certain point, age and death are indistinguishable. And he did not want to cheat even Number 1 of the solemnity that should attend the moment of death.

He sat apart from her on the moulded plastic bench of the alcove, trying not to stare at her. Seen against this whiteness, in this sourceless, glaring light, each component of her physical being presented itself to him with unnatural clarity: the series of tiny metal spheres buttoning up the cracked black leather of her high shoes; the folds of the crepe, the crisp little puckers where it was gathered at the neck and shoulders, the flounces drooping at the ends of the long sleeves; the thin strands of white hair falling across her waxen forehead; the yellow tinct of her fingers, whitening where age had drawn the flesh taut across the bones; the wrinkled face.

The wrinkles: these above all. Her face had become a pretext for these wrinkles. Unless he made a special effort, all the rest–eyes, mouth, nose, etc.–would blur and varnish into the generality, to become mere special instances of Wrinkliness.

"You have been waiting for this moment a long time, Number 2." Her manner toward him was at once warm and distant, as though beneath each simple cordial banality there lurked depths of significance which it were better most of the world should remain in ignorance of, but which she would reveal to him.

"Yes, a long time," he said, safely.

"Perhaps you'd even given up hope." A statement, not a question, but spoken in such an ineffable tone that it might have meant anything. He was to infer that she lived in those lofty regions where all opposites are resolved into Oneness.

He refused to make the inference, and replied to her statement as though it had been a question. "No. In fact, it was more than just a hope. I always knew this moment was inevitable for us."

"For us!" He seemed not to understand that this was to have been his moment, not theirs, the moment of his fulfillment, a gift from the infinite One to the finite Two.

"Us, certainly. Here we are, after all this time, actually confronting each other, face to face." He stared directly into the wrinkles, where one thin line amid the calligraphic maze formed what on another face would have been a smile.

"Such a strange way you have, Number 2, of putting it–a confrontation!"

"Yes, that's the sort of thing I'd have said before my conversion."

"Exactly what I had thought."

"Why *am* I here?"

"Should you have to *ask*, Number 2? Isn't it enough to *be* here?"

"Here–in this room?"

"Here, with me. Why all these questions? Can it be so hard to look at old Granny in this new light?"

He ignored her question to ask his own: "Do you *live* here, in this room?"

She ignored his to ask *her* own: "Do you like it?" She waved a regal hand at the bright void before them, quite as though it contained a boutique's worth of particulars for his admiration and applause: bouquets of hair-flowers under glass bells, a collection of her finest red and white embroidered roses, albums of photographs, a cast-iron chandelier.

"It's very plain," he said noncommitally.

"But it's a plainness that *suits* me."

"Oh yes," he agreed, "it does that."

"One grows tired of ostentation more quickly than of plainness." She employed "One" not as an impersonal pronoun but as a monarch would refer to himself as "We."

"In principle I agree, though in practice I think that plainness can be carried too far."

The old woman rose from the "window-seat," wringing her hands in agitation. She followed a zigzagging path across the room, as though for her there were obstacles everywhere. She looked all about, focusing on one particular point in this void after another. "I wish," she said (becoming, for the nonce, helpless, vague old Grandmother Bug), "you'd *tell* me what it is! These *hints* will drive me out of my mind. If there's something you don't like, then for pity's sake, say what it is, and I'll have them take it *away*!" She removed from one ruffled sleeve a lace handkerchief, in case she found herself obliged to cry.

He could not decide if the Empress really believed herself to be clothed. "There's no one thing I could point to," he said carefully. "It's a more general impression. Perhaps it's only that I'm not *used* to it."

This seemed to satisfy her, for she tucked the handkerchief back up her sleeve.

"Oh, but you will *grow* used to it," she assured him sweetly, and it was then, for the first time, for the only time, that he experienced true terror, the terror he had glimpsed in other Villagers, that had been occasioned, for them too, by something as disproportionate, as ludicrously mild as these few words, spoken so warmly, with such a gentle refinement. "Oh, but you will *grow* used to it."

"No. I won't."

One could not doubt his conviction. "No?" she asked, without a doubt.

"It just isn't to my *taste*."

"Really?" She returned to the alcove, as the crow flies, straight at him. "Am *I* to your taste, then?" she insisted, thrusting the crumpled parchment of her face into his smooth vellum.

A smell of musk issued from the wrinkles.

By an effort of the will he did not draw back, nor could anything more be read on the vellum than a certain bland befuddlement. "In what *sense*, Number 1?"

She withdrew the parchment. His mere utterance of her number seemed to reassure her. Remembering to be Granny, she seated herself, folded her venerable hands in her lap, smoothed out the parchment to show that it had actually been a generous Bequest, to which she now added, as a kind of codicil, a smile, while her eyes, unsmiling, preserved a clause of *in terro rem*.

"Dear, dear Number 2," old Granny said, leaving no doubt that dear, dear Number 2 was expected to reply in kind. When he did not, she added a second log to this blaze of affection: "I wish there were *something* I could do for *you*."

He *should* have said: "It's enough that you allow me to serve your cause." And further rhapsodies on that theme.

He *did* say: "There is. You could answer some questions that have been troubling me for quite some time."

The hands awoke in her lap and disarranged themselves. "Questions! Oh dear. Are you sure you want to ask them of *me*? I'm very bad at questions."

"There's no one else who can answer the questions I have in mind."

"That's very likely," she said. "But even so!"

"What is the purpose of this Village, Number 1?"

"Purpose? Village? Such an odd question. Villages don't have purposes–they have *people*."

"The purpose of this organization, then."

Again Granny rose and walked to the middle of the white room, as though, being far-sighted, she could only observe him closely from this distance. "Organization is *such* an ugly word. Though I suppose it's to the point. What is the purpose of *any* organization, Number 2? To grow. And to exist. We want to grow as much as we can, to exist as long as we can. And, though it's not for *me* to say so, I think we can be proud of ourselves, of all that we've done so far in these two respects. Though we can't slacken *now*."

"How long has the Village been here? When did the organization begin to *exist*?"

She tapped her lips with a bony index finger, frowning. And sighed. "I'm sorry, but I have such a terrible head for dates. I hope that wasn't one of the *important* questions."

"Did you come to this Village? Or did you *make* it?"

"I made it." With a modest smile, as though she had been praised once again for her wonderful pineapple upside-down cake.

"You–who *are* you?"

"But you can *see* me, Number 2! I am what I appear to be, neither more nor less." She shook her head at the absurdity of having to explain anything so obvious: "I'm Number 1."

A memory, from the farthest darkness of his past: of riding in a school-bus at night, sitting alone in a double seat. While he stared at the hypnotic flicker of the white lines on the highway, the other boys had sung an endless refrain of: "We're here because we're here because we're here because . . ."

He wondered if, after all, there was no other explanation for the Village than that: because it was here. Possibly at one time it had possessed a purpose, but over the years that purpose had been forgotten, or lost. Indeed, Number 1, as she threaded her way through the private labyrinth of the empty white room, seemed to be pantomiming some kind of search: she lifted cushions, peeked behind clocks, examined dusty shelves, looking for something she was certain she'd misplaced, though she had forgotten what that had been. Her spectacles perhaps? Her embroidery hoop? Her teeth?

And then–of course!–she found it in the pocket of her dress: her platinum buttonhook!

"You can answer this much, at least," he demanded. "Who *runs* the Village? Who makes its laws? Who judges us?"

"I do, Number 2," she said sternly. "Your questions become less and less necessary."

"Bear with me–I don't have many more. *How* do you do it?"

She stared at the notched tip of the buttonhook, frowning the wrinkles into a pattern of vexation. "By delegating authority, Number 2. By delegating it to *you*."

"*Why*? Why me? Why did you want *me* to become Number 2?"

"I didn't *want* it. You *are* Number 2. Now–have you *finished* with these silly questions, and may *I* say something to *you*?"

Was he ready to admit defeat? He had not in any case expected to win this part of the contest. It was time, therefore, to proceed to the second part, which (he smiled grimly) he *would* win.

Number 1, interpreting the smile as his consent, began to shake the platinum buttonhook at him energetically. "Number 2, 1 must say that I have been very disappointed with you today, very disappointed *indeed*! Your attitude suggests to me that your conversion has been anything but—"

She saw the tensing of the thigh, the shift of his torso. She raised the buttonhook to her mouth and bit down firmly on the notched end.

But not, by a nanosecond, soon enough. He had already sprung forward from the bench, out of the alcove, when the sound wave of the implosion crashed about the room.

He raised himself from the white, unshadowed floor, blinked sight back into his eyes. Number 1 stood by the far wall of the room, fondling the buttonhook.

Behind him, where the alcove had been, a perfect rectangle of blackness negated the middle third of the wall.

"I should like to know, Number 2, what it is you think you're doing?"

"And I'd like to know what you did."

"Stay away from me! Stay away, or I'll do it again!" She raised the buttonhook threateningly, but his step did not falter. There were no more alcoves now, and she would not spring the jaws of any trap in which she might be caught as well.

"Wall!" she shouted. "*Wall*!" She beat soundlessly with the end of the buttonhook against the unyielding white plane. Then, without a flicker of transition, the four walls, the ceiling, the floor, everything but the rectangle of blackness that had replaced the alcove, was transformed into something stranger than emptiness. Beneath him there was no longer the level floor but a rolling trembling mass of pinks and violets, veined with writhing tendrils of gray, flecked, like the ocean, with milk-white clusters of foam, that burst, that bubbled up afresh. The walls and ceiling too had metamorphosed into the same composite of animal and vegetable forms-vastly enlarged inner organs that slid among even vaster petals. Yet his feet, for all that they seemed set upon nothing but this heaving pink stew, gripped the floor as securely as before.

An illusion, as usual.

Number 1 continued to pound soundlessly upon the soundless swarm of shapes, continued to call out, hysterically: "Wall! Wall!"

He caught hold of the hand that grasped the buttonhook. Her struggles were feeble as a child's. She glared at him with the swift, all-engulfing hatred of an infant powerless despite the conviction of his own omnipotence.

"Don't you *dare*!" she screamed at him. "Don't you—"

With a dry snap her hand broke off at the wrist. Her mouth gaped, and she uttered a cry, a quick inward gasp, of horror and outraged modesty. She ceased, in any way, to struggle.

At once the pulsing images about them receded, condensing into vivid squares, like single marble tiles set in the middle of each white plane.

The hand on the white floor slowly spread open its fingers. They could both see, where the skin had been frayed at the knuckles by the buttonhook, the tangle of tubes and wires that had made it work.

Her wrist, where the hand had broken off, gave out a

buzz that resembled the "engaged" signal a telephone makes, but higher-pitched, a humming, like the humming of a children's chorus, a great mass of voices, heard from a great distance, that rose, by swift octaves, out of the audible range.

Chapter Twenty

Much Adieus

Granny held up the stump of her wrist and looked at it curiously. "For heaven's sake!" she said. "Did you *ever*?"

A second rectangle of blackness had formed opposite the first: the guillotine had been raised to admit a squad, two squads of guards. They entered with great purposefulness, but the scene that confronted them in the white room did not suggest any definite course of action. They coagulated in a circle about the detached hand, one finger of which still twitched erratically.

One guard bent over and picked up the platinum buttonhook. He offered it first to Number 2, who declined it with a shake of his head, then to the old woman, who reached out for it, unthinkingly, with the same arm from which hand and buttonhook had just been removed.

She tisked, bethought herself, accepted the buttonhook with the hand left to her, and placed it in her pocket, where it belonged.

"Oh dear," she said. "Oh, dear, it *is* a nuisance. And just when everything had been going so *nicely*. I do hope you will *excuse*–" She tried to indicate the unmentionable object on the floor without in any crude way *pointing* to it.

"I'm certain I don't know *who* . . . In all this confusion–"

She turned imploringly to the one man in the room who seemed to be a gentleman: "If you'd be so kind as to bring me that *chair*? My legs, you know, are not all that they were."

The guards, gathering courage, had picked up the hand from the floor, and were passing it about their circle.

The doctor appeared at the threshold of the room, a white figure framed by the blackness, a painting on velvet. "That will be *quite* enough!" she said to the startled guards. Had she shaken a caduceus at them, she could not have presented a more fearful image of the authority of Medical Science. She pointed to the hand. "Put that back where you found it, and then leave this room so that we can . . ." Her powers of improvisation flagging, she looked to him for help.

"So that we can discuss what must be *done* now," he said, with an authority (viceregal) to equal hers. "Quickly, please, this is a crisis!"

When they were by themselves, it was the old woman who spoke first. "Would . . . a cup of tea . . . be too much trouble?" With the loss of her hand, she seemed to have reverted completely from her character as Number 1 to the less demanding role of Grandmother Bug. "With just a *drop* . . . of milk . . . and one lump . . ."

"What happened?" Number 14 asked, trying to catch a look at the stump, which was veiled discreetly by a flounce of crepe.

"A malfunction, it seems."

"Oh, but she's not—" The doctor placed her hand above Granny's sagging bosom, to be sure. "She has a *heart*," she said surely.

"Or something."

"You can *feel* it, beating."

"I'd rather not."

Granny, whimpering, sought to retain the interest of this pretty lady with white hair. "My dear, if you would just lend me your *arm* a minute . . . it isn't very far at all. And I'm feeling so—" She shook her head. "And, in short, my dear, not at all *myself.*"

"In a moment, Granny, we'll have you in a nice warm bed."

"Will we?" he asked doubtfully.

"Do you have another suggestion?"

He looked at Granny, at the hand that the guard had replaced on the floor, at the doctor, at Granny. Even if she *were* a robot, she commanded a degree of sympathy in her reduced state, and the doctor seemed persuaded that she was (at least partially) human.

A voice in a peculiar bass register, as though a tape were being played at too slow a speed, addressed them from the whiteness all around: "I wish to announce that in the event of the demise" (slowing still more, to the croaking of a giant frog) "of Nummboor Onnne thaat mmmeaszhoorzz haave" (and speeding, rising quickly from frog, to bass, to tenor, to soprano) "been taken to assure the certain annihilation of this Village and of—" It ended in a squeal of slate, a squeak of flute.

"That seems to decide it." Number 14 stooped, with a sigh, to retrieve the hand on the floor. "I had better see if I can reassemble this. Damn! Now you'll have to run off before we've had a single moment to ourselves."

"I will? As quickly as all that?"

"We wouldn't want the world, or whatever, to blow up on *our* account."

"The old girl is still on her feet. She seems to be in no *immediate* danger of dying."

"Well, until I know how she's been ... put together, *I* wouldn't give a prognosis. Besides, she could come out of shock at any moment, and you should be gone before she starts feeling 'like herself' again. That funny little mute servant of yours is waiting outside with your car."

"Quicker and quicker."

"Oh, I've had him on hand since you were decanted from the tank."

"I must thank you for that, you know."

"I was waiting to be thanked."

"Thank you, Number 14, for your sabotage."

"You're welcome. Do you know, this whole last month while you've been Number 2–and such a dreadful scoutmaster of a Number 2 you were!–I was horribly afraid that I hadn't disconnected the right wires. In the past I was always able to rely on Number 28 for such things. I feared that you had metamorphosed in earnest. Your acting was that good that I could never be certain."

"And I was never certain at what point I'd been taken from the tank. Those dreams were every bit as real as you said they would be. Much realer than *this*."

She regarded the nothingness about them thoughtfully. "Who's to say this is real? It doesn't have the *earmarks* of reality. I'm sure that so long as you remain in the Village, you'll remain in some doubt. But once you've been in London a week or so everything will begin to look firmer and more trustworthy."

"Including yourself?"

"I won't be there, Number . . . I don't know what number to call you anymore!"

"Then why—"

"Do favors for you, if I won't be there to reap a benefit? Because, as I've said so often, I *love* you. But I know you don't believe that, even now. Leave the Village. Prove to yourself that you're *free.* Then, if for any reason you should *want* to see me again, I'll still be here. Waiting."

"Like bait in a trap?"

"You forget that you're still Number 2, officially. You can come and go as you like."

"Not once Granny's been restored to her old self."

"Well, it has to be done. I believe what that recording said. It's altogether feasible. A trigger of that kind, that's released by death, can be installed these days, at any large hospital, as easily as a car radio. If it were only a matter of the Village, I might say to hell with it, but Number 1 would have wanted a much larger blaze of glory than that. I feel I should do what I can. But as to Granny's wanting to be revenged on you, I think I've had enough practice fiddling the dials in people's heads that I can persuade her that things happened somewhat differently than they did. She'll believe that she's sent you off on some nebulous but absolutely essential *mission.* So, if you *do* begin to feel nostalgic . . ."

"*If* I do, I'll come back. But it's a damned small *if* to rest any hope on."

"Then I'll have learned not to gamble so recklessly next time. You do think better of me now, don't you, than you did at first? Allow me that much."

"Oh, I'd allow a lot more than that. Even then, though, the problem remains just how much you may have fiddled my dials."

"It can't be helped, my dear. That problem always remains, once you start this kind of thing going. Dr Johnson had the best solution: go kick a stone, and let the stone prove to your foot that they're *both* real."

She turned over Granny's hand palm-upward and ran her fingernail across the exposed tubes and wires. "At least in *most* cases that's the best solution," she added with a small sad smile that was intended only for herself. She steered the old woman by one bony rudder of shoulder toward the black threshold.

Granny turned around in the doorway, a spark of intelligence rekindling in her eyes. "I remember now! I remember what it was I had to say!"

Neither of them would ask her what it was she had remembered.

"Young man," she said, in her loftiest voice, "you make a *wretched* cup of tea!"